Never Say Goodbye

A SMALL TOWN CHRISTIAN ROMANCE

UNFAILING LOVE
BOOK TWO

MANDI BLAKE

Never Say Goodbye
Unfailing Love Book 2
By Mandi Blake

Copyright © 2019 Mandi Blake
All Rights Reserved.

No part of this book may be used or reproduced in any manner whatsoever without written permission, except in the case of brief quotations embedded in critical articles and reviews. The unauthorized reproduction or distribution of this copyrighted work is illegal. No part of this book may be scanned, uploaded or distributed via the Internet or any other means, electronic or print, without the author's permission.

This book is a work of fiction. The names, characters, places, and incidents are products of the writer's imagination or have been used fictitiously and are not to be construed as real. Any resemblance to persons, living or dead, actual events, locale or organizations is entirely coincidental. The author does not have any control over and does not assume any responsibility for third-party websites or their content.

Published in the United States of America

Cover Designer: Amanda Walker PA & Design Services

Editor: Editing Done Write

Contents

1. Lindsey — 1
2. Dakota — 8
3. Lindsey — 13
4. Lindsey — 21
5. Dakota — 30
6. Lindsey — 42
7. Lindsey — 50
8. Dakota — 61
9. Lindsey — 72
10. Dakota — 81
11. Lindsey — 86
12. Dakota — 99
13. Lindsey — 107
14. Dakota — 115
15. Lindsey — 126
16. Dakota — 138
17. Lindsey — 146
18. Lindey — 153
19. Dakota — 162
20. Lindsey — 170
21. Lindsey — 175
22. Dakota — 188
23. Lindsey — 201
24. Lindsey — 208
25. Lindsey — 217
26. Lindsey — 226
27. Dakota — 234

28. Lindsey	242
29. Dakota	251
30. Lindsey	259
31. Lindsey	275
Other Books By Mandi Blake	281
About the Author	285
Acknowledgments	287
Note from the Author	289
Living Hope	291

CHAPTER 1
Lindsey

Lindsey didn't want to be here. Carson, Georgia was the last place she wanted to be, yet here she was driving into town like it was no big deal.

It was definitely a big deal, if only to her.

Her sweaty hands slipped on the steering wheel of her trusty old Maxima. She stopped at the only traffic light in town and shook her hands before drying them on her faded blue jeans. Her sweaty hands were gross, but she was having trouble keeping herself together. She did *not* want to be here.

Actually, she *shouldn't* be here, and that was the reason her gut was telling her to turn around. She had caused enough pain in this quiet town, and she didn't want to face it. Not now, and not ever. She wanted to pretend it hadn't happened. Staying away, saving the people she'd hurt from what she could still do to them, was a gift.

Lindsey drove slowly through town as she hit all of the stop signs. The town was just as cute and quaint as she remembered. She hadn't been here in years, and this place felt frozen in time. The shops and restaurants along the streets hadn't changed their signs or logos. Even the flowers along the sidewalk looked the same.

How had she left this place? Her heart went out to the small town, and the nostalgia almost allowed her to forget that she didn't belong here. Everything about this town was the same. She was the one who had changed.

She remembered that her best friend, Sissy, had asked—no, begged her to come. She loved Sissy with all of her heart and then some, but she hadn't been strong enough to come back here until now.

Sissy was having a baby and had asked Lindsey to be here for the birth. In another life, that was fair and understandable. She would never even think of missing the birth of her friend's daughter. Somehow, life had become so mixed up and cruel along the way, and she had debated telling her friend she couldn't come.

How had she ever considered ditching her friend? She loved Sissy, and the woman would do anything for her. Lindsey owed this to Sissy in a multitude of ways. She hated herself for being selfish enough to even think twice before rushing to her pregnant friend's side. She still couldn't believe Sissy spoke to her after what she'd done. Her friend had every right to turn her back on her. Instead, they'd never mentioned it, and Lindsey was eternally grateful.

She had only seen Sissy a handful of times in the last six years, but they talked almost every day. Sissy had visited Lindsey in the various apartments and lofts she'd lived in over the years, claiming she was in need of an adventure outside of town. She knew why Sissy never asked her to visit Carson. Her friend had known she would say no.

Lindsey thanked the stars often that Sissy and her husband, Tyler, had eloped and she hadn't been invited to a hometown wedding. Just thinking of the ulcers that would have induced made her blood pressure rise.

Now, as she sucked in deep breaths to avoid a panic attack, she wondered again how badly this would turn out. What were the chances she wouldn't see *him* or any of his friends and she could slink out of here without making waves?

She wished again, for the millionth time, that things had turned out differently all those years ago. They had a chance, and she blew it. She hadn't made the right decisions, hadn't followed the right dream, hadn't fought for the right passion. Hindsight was 20/20, and she saw things all too clearly now.

Lindsey had been wrong. She knew that now, but there was no way she could go back. She couldn't right the wrongs, and now she just had to maintain until she could get away from here again.

Things couldn't get any worse, right?

Her phone rang in the console beside her and she answered it while navigating a four-way stop.

"Hey, Mom. Sorry I forgot to call, but I made it into town."

"Good, sweetie. How are you managing?" Her mom, Kathy, was sympathetic of her apprehensions for this place to an extent.

"I'm... making it. Just ready to see my friend and her sweet baby so I can get this behind me." Lindsey stopped in front of a diner that she had always loved and remembered when they'd eaten there every Saturday morning.

Stop. She'd promised herself she wouldn't think about him *or* the things they used to do together while she was in town. Releasing a shaky breath, she accelerated through the intersection and away from the memory.

"Please try to enjoy it while you're there. You have a week off from work. You shouldn't be stressing. Leave that tension at work."

Her mother certainly tried to say all the right things, but her mom would never understand that Lindsey loved her job. It wasn't stressful. It was relaxing to be able to do something she was good at all day and get paid for it. She was slowly working her way out of debt, so she felt like things were on the mend. Doing something with her life that was constant and productive felt better than the uncertainty of the entertainment industry she left behind.

Her mom also couldn't understand what it meant to work for a living. Her mom had lived and thrived under her dad's wing until they divorced a few years ago. Lindsey's parents had married young, and she didn't think her mother had ever been employed.

They hadn't been wealthy by any stretch of the imagination, but her dad had supported them almost too well. His career was his life, and it had driven a wedge between her parents for as long as she could remember. Once Lindsey was out on her own, her parents had amicably gone their separate ways.

Doubt bubbled up as she struggled to remember where the hotel she intended to stay at was located, and she was beginning to second-guess herself. Bernard's Hotel might not even be in business anymore. Maybe she should've studied up on the directions before the drive.

As she turned onto another unfamiliar street, she looked around and realized she was too distracted by the phone call with her mother to be driving.

She craned her neck to check the road name as she passed it. "Thanks, Mom. I'll call you when I—"

Lindsey turned back to face the road ahead of her and saw a broad-shouldered man standing only feet in front of her car. Her foot pummeled the brake pedal in an effort to stop before she hit him, and she dropped the phone. She now noticed that her vehicle was surrounded by traffic cones and shiny, orange construction barrels. When she took a second to breathe, the man slammed his palms onto the hood of her car, commanding her attention.

"What are you doing?" he shouted. "You almost hit me. I'm pretty hard to miss." He threw his arms out at his sides to emphasize the fact that he *was* large and hard to miss, just as he claimed. Not to even mention the safety vest he wore. She really hadn't been paying attention, and her face grew hot.

But now she was stunned. Speechless. Because she saw his face and prayed her eyes were deceiving her.

No, no, no. This was worse than she could have imagined. It couldn't be him. Surely, life wasn't that cruel.

"What are you staring at?" he yelled at her, and his voice still held the sting of his anger.

She heard a small squeak from the phone that had landed in the passenger seat and jumped for it.

"Mom, I'm so sorry. I'll call you later. Love you." She spat the words quickly and hung up the phone. Could it be possible that he didn't recognize her? Maybe there was still time to make an escape.

She remembered that she did look very different now than she had six years ago when she last saw him. She decided to use this to her advantage and pray that he forgot all about the crazy lady who almost ran him over with her car.

She pressed the button to open her window barely an inch and tilted her head to speak out the gap. "I'm sorry. I wasn't paying attention. I'll just get out of your way." Her voice was shaky, but she hoped he would just let it go since she had expressed her apologies.

She saw the change in his face as soon as she finished speaking. It was a look of recognition, and his brows pulled together as he squinted to see through her windshield. "Hold up…"

He stalked toward her driver's side window, and she panicked. She threw the car into reverse and backed out of the street to the intersection. She was thankful there were no other cars around because she was being completely reckless, again. She decided any street was better than this one as she sped away from Dakota Calhoun, the man who held her heart and haunted her dreams.

CHAPTER 2
Dakota

Dakota watched her car speed away from him and rubbed the back of his sweaty neck. There was no way that was her, right? He hadn't seen or heard from Lindsey in years, and there was no way she would be caught here again. Lindsey Payne had bigger and better places to be.

No, Little Lindsey didn't belong in Carson. She'd made that clear when she left. She was meant for bright lights and sleepless streets, and Carson was too small town for her big dreams.

Or maybe *he* just hadn't been good enough for her.

He shook his head to dispel the thoughts. He knew he wasn't good enough for her, but he'd given her everything he had just for her to say it wasn't enough. She'd left anyway, and he had all but begged her to stay. He knew she didn't want to stay in Carson, but he had wanted her to stay with him, whatever it took.

Nothing had been enough, and now he couldn't

help the feeling that the voice he just heard was the one he hadn't been able to get out of his head for six years.

He pulled his cell out of his pocket and called the one person who would be able to answer his questions.

"Hey, brother bear." His sister's voice was always too chipper for his taste as she answered the call.

"Sissy, is there someone in town I should know about?" He would give his sister a chance to give it to him straight. Hopefully, she would think he could handle the truth, even if he wasn't sure himself.

"No." Her reply was clipped and matter of fact. It was also a blatant lie.

"Come on, Sissy, stop playing games and tell me the truth. Is Lindsey here? I think I just saw her, and I'm not in the mood for this. Stop acting like a..."

A baby. That's why Lindsey would be here. Sissy's baby was due any day now, and of course, her best friend would be here for the birth. He rubbed the bridge of his nose and cursed himself for not seeing this coming. He could have at least prepared to see Lindsey again. Instead, he'd been blindsided and lost his temper the first time he saw her in over half a decade.

Losing control of his temper with Lindsey wasn't something that had happened often. They'd always been close enough to understand each other even when times were tough. The one time they hadn't been on the same page had been enough to break them.

Lindsey had always been able to read his thoughts,

his moods, and his temperament when they were young. They'd spent all of their time together and had been so consumed by each other that they often forgot who and where they were, and were too drunk on love to give a care about anything but each other.

He kicked the sidewalk with the steel toe of his boot and reminded himself that what he and Lindsey had back then was first love and impossible to replicate.

He also told himself, again, that it was over.

Would Lindsey always have this control over him? He hated it now just as much as he had when she left, and he still hadn't managed to shake the hold she had on him. She'd only crossed his mind a few hundred times this week, and they were six years into their eternal separation.

"Never mind. I guess I just figured it out. She's here to see Lydia, isn't she?" he asked.

"Of course not." Sissy sounded offended. "She's here to see me, and Lydia will be a cute, little bonus."

He sighed, "I would've appreciated a heads up, Sis."

"I know, but I didn't know how to tell you. I love you both, and I've always hated being in the middle. I know she wouldn't have wanted you to know, and telling you felt like it would hurt you too." Sissy was the most caring and understanding sister he could have asked for, and he hated that her friendship with Lindsey had suffered because of the breakup.

"I get it, Sis. I just... need some time to wrap my head around seeing her again. It's like she brings out the worst in me now. I don't know if I can keep it together around her." He kicked the sidewalk again to release some of his mounting frustration. "I need to get back to work so I'll be caught up when Lydia comes. I'm gonna try to take a week off when she's born."

He was secretly ecstatic for the arrival of his niece, but he was careful to keep his emotions tempered on the subject of family. He wanted what Sissy had found more than anything. He wanted the house, the kids, the family life.

He wanted a wife, but those dreams were shattered when Lindsey left. That's when he realized that he only wanted those things with *her*. No one else would do, and he didn't have any desire to have a family if Lindsey wasn't part of the equation.

"Aww you love us," she crooned. "You really do have a heart. Say you're excited." Sissy talked fast when she was on a roll.

His tone grew serious again. "I'm not ready to see her, Sis. I know I'll have to soon, but—"

He was talking when Sissy interrupted with a hissing intake of breath through her teeth.

"What was that?" Dakota asked in monotone fear as his steps halted.

There was a moment of silence before she responded. "I had a contraction. I had a contraction! My first contraction!" Why did she sound excited? He'd always been led to believe that contractions were the most painful thing a human could experience. He would never understand Sissy. His heart beat double time at the admission.

"What does that mean? Is it time? Do I need to come pick you up?" He melted into a business attitude and waited for directions.

"No, but maybe that means Lydia will be here soon." She squealed. "I'm so excited. I have to go call Tyler."

"Wait. Keep me posted. I'll wrap things up here until I hear from you." He was already walking back to his rig.

"Okay. I'll call. Promise."

"Hey, Sis. You're going to be a great mom. Love you."

"Kota, you can't say things like that to a pregnant lady. My emotions don't work right because of these stupid hormones." Her voice was thick with emotion. "I love you too."

He hung up the phone and felt equal parts anticipation and resentment. He was excited to be an uncle, but he was selfish enough to be jealous of the happiness his sister had found in her growing family.

As he made his way back into the construction site, he forced his thoughts away from the frustrating Lindsey and back into business.

CHAPTER 3
Lindsey

Her heart was still beating like a jackhammer when she pulled up at Sissy and Tyler's house. She hadn't visited Sissy since she and Tyler bought a house together, but she knew the house all too well. It was the same historical estate that she and Sissy had drooled over as teens. Now, she and Sissy spoke frequently about how lucky Sissy was to be living there.

They'd spent many sleepovers lying side by side imagining what the inside of the most beautiful house in Carson might look like. Sissy imagined a bright entryway with bluestone floors that highlighted the light-limestone staircase spindles. Lindsey thought the interior would be made up of warm, dim rooms trimmed in gold accents and mahogany tables.

Sissy had refused to tell her what the house actually looked like after she moved in with Tyler, explaining that only a visit would reveal the secret.

Lindsey had given up on finding the hotel and driven to the one place she really wanted to be. She wanted to hug her friend after their months apart and really needed the comfort after almost literally running into Dakota.

Pulling into the circle drive in front of the home that could only be described as a mansion, Lindsey gawked at her friend's place. Tall white columns framed the front entrance, and weeping ferns hung at intervals along the porch between them.

Oh, how the status gap had widened between the two of them over the years. She never resented her friend for being successful in her interior design business or marrying a prominent doctor, but she felt the distance more clearly now than ever since she'd moved away from Carson. Once again, the knife twisted in her gut that reminded her of that terrible decision she made all those years ago.

Sissy came from a family centered on helping others, and she'd picked up the torch with ease. Sissy never wasted an opportunity to help someone in need, and it was fitting that she found love with a doctor who had the gift of healing.

Sissy's mother was a pharmacist, and her father had been a preacher. Her mother was the breadwinner and her father the soul winner, and they'd flourished together.

When Sissy's father died when they were so young, the whole town had mourned. He was loved by all and had sat at the bedside of almost every townsperson in sickness or injury at one time or another. Lindsey had no doubt that Sissy's father would be proud if he could see her now. Not by her wealth, but he would see her heart, and he would know it was filled with goodness and giving. He would rest easy knowing Sissy lived a life for God and gave so much of herself to others.

Lindsey released a tense breath and rang the ornate, yet modern doorbell that should have been out of place on this ancient house but fit surprisingly well. Sissy always had a knack for decorating, and she could see things others couldn't bring to life. Lindsey waited a minute, and after hearing nothing was about to ring again when the door swung open abruptly.

Sissy was always shining and bright, but now she looked tired. Lindsey could only imagine how exhausting pregnancy could be and simply smiled at her friend.

"Ahh, stranger! I'm glad you're finally here!" Sissy screamed. The exhausted look from the moment before had vanished. Sissy grabbed her into the best hug she could manage with the baby belly between them. "Get your butt in here. You're just in time." Sissy pulled her into the entryway by her arm, and Lindsey gave a small amount of resistance as she gaped at the open space.

It was just as Sissy had described all those years ago. A blue-and-white marble effect coursed through the room reminding her of a glass ocean. Sissy was living in her dream house, but she'd made it the home of her imagination.

"Sissy, it's beautiful. It's better than I imagined. You have an incredible talent." Lindsey was still observing the room in awe.

"Come on, lady, we have work to do," Sissy called, and Lindsey realized she had been left at the bottom of the stairs. Sissy was quick for a waddling pregnant woman.

She followed Sissy's chatter to a room upstairs that could only be the master bedroom, which was cavernous but comfortable. The carpet was thick and the four-poster king bed was covered in a dozen strewn pillows and a thick comforter. The floor was littered with clothing and various toiletries that surrounded an open suitcase. Sissy was bustling around moving things from one place to another.

"You aren't packed yet? I could've sworn Tyler would've made sure that was finished weeks ago," Lindsey joked. Tyler was the planner and the worrier. Sissy was carefree and flew by the seat of her pants.

"Oh, it's packed. I'm just adding the last few things, like my toothbrush and stuff." Sissy crammed a few more things into the bursting suitcase and zipped it up.

Lindsey took the suitcase from her friend as Sissy awkwardly stood, cradling her round belly in one hand and bracing her back with the other. "Where do you want to put this?" Lindsey asked.

Sissy bent slightly and sucked in air around her teeth. "In the car."

Lindsey's brow furrowed as she asked, "Is that a contraction? Did it just start?"

"I've been having them for about fifteen minutes, and they aren't bad yet, but Tyler wanted me to get ready when I called to tell him. He said it usually takes a while with the first, but you know he always thinks better safe than sorry. He's on his way home now."

Lindsey was all smiles. "I can't believe this is happening. I'm so excited."

"I was actually on the phone with Dakota when it started." Sissy gave her a quizzical look. "He thought he'd seen a ghost."

Lindsey's embarrassment was back and she could feel her cheeks heating. "Well, it would've been hard to miss me since I almost hit him with my car."

Sissy broke into an uninhibited laugh. "What? You're kidding. I have to hear this story."

"There isn't much to tell. I was looking for the old Bernard Hotel and got a little lost. I wasn't paying attention to the road, and he was there when I turned around. I think he was wearing a safety vest in a construction zone. Is he working in construction now?" she asked innocently.

"You could say that. He stays busy, so he usually has a couple of jobs on the books at any point in time," Sissy replied. "Why don't you go get your bags, and I'll show you to your room."

"I was planning to stay at the Bernard. Is it still open?" Lindsey asked. The Bernard Hotel had been owned by a local family for almost a hundred years, and it was known far and wide for its historic appearance and hospitality.

"You are not staying at a hotel when I have a room for you. I thought that was the plan all along. I need as much time with you as I can get while you're here. I never get to see you. Plus, you're on baby call. I'm going to need your help when Lydia comes." Sissy was pouting now, and Lindsey didn't want to turn down a free room.

"I'll be right back." She grabbed her suitcase from the car and met Sissy at the top of the stairs before following her into a guest room at the opposite end of the hall from the master.

"The nursery is between us, but this room has you written all over it." Sissy smiled deviously as she entered.

Lindsey stepped into the room and couldn't believe what she was seeing. It was a picture of perfection. Three cream-colored walls were accented by one wall covered in dark wooden bookshelves surrounding a fireplace. A single ornate rug covered part of the hardwood floors. Chocolate floor-to-ceiling curtains covered in golden flowers framed a large window, and an ivory down comforter sat atop the queen bed surrounded by thick mahogany columns.

"Sissy, you really are amazing. If I ever have a house of my own, will you please decorate it for me?" Lindsey couldn't believe the beauty of the room her friend had created with her in mind.

"Don't worry. I've already decorated your house."

She gave a wink that said she had interesting things in store for Lindsey's future home.

"It's just like we talked about, but so much better," Lindsey corrected just as Sissy braced herself on the doorframe to weather a contraction.

"Have you been tracking the frequency? I downloaded an app for that before I came." Lindsey retrieved her cell from the back pocket of her jeans.

"No, but they're getting stronger." They heard a door shut downstairs and Sissy yelled, "We're upstairs, Ty."

Tyler joined them at the top of the stairs. He was tall and lean but clearly in shape. He carried himself with authority but lacked the harsh look of someone who thrived on control. His sandy blond hair was cut neat, and he wore khakis and a plaid button-down shirt.

He wasted no time with pleasantries as he approached them. "How long do they last? What are your intervals? You should be sitting." He was a volley of questions and requests as he pulled Sissy into his arms and kissed her head.

"I'm fine, worrywart." Sissy rubbed her belly and stretched her back. "However, I do think we could leisurely make our way to the hospital now because they're starting to really hurt." Sissy turned back to Lindsey as she began to make her way down the stairs. "Ty, this is Lindsey. You practically already know her."

He gave a genuine grin as he pulled Lindsey into a

hug. "Good to meet you, Lindsey. Ready to coach Miss bossy-pants into having a baby today?"

She felt like she knew Tyler already, after hearing about him for years. Sissy was lovestruck with Tyler and never missed an opportunity to croon about him, even when they had the occasional tiff, which didn't last long.

"It's great to finally meet you." They raced down the stairs after Sissy. "You think it'll happen today?" Lindsey asked.

"Possibly. You never know with the first." Tyler was trying his best to keep calm, but she could see the sweat beading on his temple.

Sissy's water broke as they passed through the kitchen, and Tyler stayed to clean it up while Lindsey ran back up the stairs to grab a change of clothes. Sissy took her time getting dressed between contractions then squeezed herself into the car. They were on the road as soon as Tyler threw the hospital bag in the back with the car seat.

"I have to call Mom and Dakota. I promised them I would call when it was really time to go," Sissy explained as she began dialing on her cell.

Lindsey was stupid to think she could avoid Dakota on this trip. His sister was having a baby after all. Now she would have to face her past and her present after their run-in earlier.

CHAPTER 4
Lindsey

Lindsey sat in the waiting room with Sissy's mother for a few hours catching up and chatting before anything happened. Barbara had always been kind to her, even after the breakup with Dakota. Lindsey had spoken to her a few times when Barbara had been with Sissy during their phone calls over the years. The spirited older woman possessed Sissy's penchant for fun.

Dakota had once been fun and adventurous, but it seemed time and maybe circumstances had hardened him. The man who stood in front of her car earlier today was not the fun man she had known, and she wondered how much she was to blame for his loss of spirit.

The waiting room began to fill as time crept on without word of Sissy or the baby. Everyone was chatting and keeping banter light, but the tension was just below the surface. They were all anxious for news.

Over the next few hours, she watched as people filed into the small waiting room and made themselves comfortable. Most people overlooked her, until someone finally stepped through the door that she knew she couldn't ignore.

Her old friend, Declan King, walked in with a tall, beautiful brunette woman at his side, and Lindsey sat up straighter in the hard hospital chair. She hadn't seen Declan in about eight years, but she would recognize him anywhere. They had all been so close before Declan joined the Army. Sissy had mentioned he was back in town and had a girlfriend, which they both found surprising. Declan had been a loner all his life, and they were both happy he'd finally found someone to share his life with.

The milling crowd parted for him as Declan crossed the room and greeted Barbara who sat only inches to her left. He didn't seem to notice her at all, and when his line of sight finally passed over Lindsey, he did a double take.

"Lindsey?" Her name was a question, and he almost sounded stunned.

"Hey, Dec." She stood to greet him with a reserved smile. She'd adored Declan once, and he'd been one of her best friends throughout her entire childhood, but things had changed between them now that were hard to ignore.

Declan was also Dakota's best friend.

"Sorry, I didn't recognize you. I'm not used to

seeing you with brown hair. It was blonde as long as I can remember." He hesitantly extended a hand to her. His face gave away nothing of his true reaction to seeing her.

"It's good to see you, and the changes go both ways, don't they?" She released his hand and pointed to his neatly trimmed beard. "Nice facial hair."

In another life, they would never have greeted each other with a formal handshake. That life didn't exist anymore, and once again she felt like she didn't belong here. Everything had changed, even her old friends.

He gave a reserved laugh and said, "Fair enough," before turning to the beautiful woman beside him and pulling her to his side snugly like a proud rooster. "This is my girlfriend, Adeline." Lindsey could feel the happiness between them and remembered all the times she'd worried that Declan's introversion might leave him lonely forever.

Lindsey gave Adeline the best smile she could muster in the midst of her own insecurities. "It's wonderful to meet you." Lindsey truly was happy to see Declan, and seeing him in love was a bonus. It gripped her heart that the chasm between herself and someone who used to be her good friend was so great. She needed friends now more than ever.

She didn't know how to express the hurt or relief she felt, so she kept it to herself. "It's a pleasure to meet you, and I'm incredibly happy for you both."

Lindsey was all smiles, until she saw the fleeting

elation on Declan's face fade. It seemed her old friend was still hiding some troubles. She'd once been able to tell Declan anything, and likewise, she and Sissy were the only girls he felt comfortable talking to back then.

Now, she knew he was hiding something from her, but she also had no right to demand he open up to her. They were strangers now, and a quick run-in wouldn't change that.

She was about to attempt to regain the light-hearted tone of their conversation when Declan's gaze was drawn to the door. She turned too, hoping Tyler would be entering to give an update on Sissy and the baby. Instead, she stood paralyzed as Dakota marched into the room.

He was considerably larger than she remembered. His chest and arms seemed huge. His black hair was wet from a recent shower, and his clothes were clean and simple, unlike the dirty work clothes he'd worn earlier today when she'd embarrassed herself beyond belief. Those light-blue eyes she'd always loved were a stark contrast to his tanned skin.

The mere sight of him sent her emotions into overdrive. The way he walked into a room—demanding attention, dragging the air from her lungs—none of it was fair. The sound of his heavy work boots thudding across the room echoed the beating of her heart.

He shook hands with a few people standing closer to the entrance. She stood frozen and barely breathing, and she could tell Declan did the same as Dakota spared a smile for his friend and took one carefree step toward them before noticing her.

Dakota's face changed and fell as the pieces clicked into place and Declan murmured, "I'll be right back," before leaving her with Adeline to head him off.

Lindsey watched as Declan ushered Dakota out the door before she could process what had nearly happened. She could only suppose Declan, ever the middle man, meant to keep the peace today for Sissy's sake.

She turned to Adeline, a little embarrassed. "I'm sorry. Dakota and I used to date, and I guess..." She didn't know how to explain this to Adeline. The uncertainty, the way her middle seemed to drop at the mention of his name, the effect he still had on her emotions. It was a life story. How could it be summed up so quickly?

"I know. Declan told me." Adeline didn't sound accusing or judgmental. Lindsey could've sworn she heard pity in her voice.

"Declan mentioned me before?" Declan had been Dakota's best friend and she his girlfriend, but they hadn't influenced each other's lives in almost a decade.

Adeline gestured to a corner of the waiting room containing a few empty seats. "You left some ripples here when you moved away. I think they lasted longer than anyone expected."

Lindsey sat down beside Declan's girlfriend and felt guilty again. She hated knowing she'd hurt someone here, especially the one she had loved so much. Now, she was getting the impression she'd left scars in unlikely places. Lindsey looked at her hands, wishing she could be anywhere else. "I didn't mean to hurt anyone, Adeline."

Adeline placed a firm hand on Lindsey's shoulder, catching her attention. "I know, and you can call me Addie."

Lindsey turned to see the woman's attention trained on the door.

"I think I understand more than I should. I've thought about your decision many times, and I can almost see why you chose the way you did." Addie paused as if she didn't know if she should continue.

"Declan and I met in an unconventional way, and we're still learning about each other. I don't have the history with him that you have with Dakota, so I can't understand that part of your story. However, I can relate to your desire to be free and chase your dreams."

Lindsey could feel the pain of the past in Addie's voice as she spoke. This stranger was opening up to her when people she'd known her whole life were shutting her out. She reached for Addie's hand that rested on her shoulder and was met with a returning squeeze.

"My ex-boyfriend basically kept me locked up for years. Declan helped me break away from him, then he helped me find myself." Addie choked on the end of her sentence, and Lindsey's throat constricted with emotion.

"I had never had a job. I had never had a hobby or a passion. Now I'm studying to become a hairdresser, and I couldn't imagine a job I would love more. Brian is teaching me to play guitar, and he lets me sing with him around town when he plays. I've even been able to sing at church once or twice. I was never able to chase my dreams, and I admire you for making a choice that was for you and you alone."

Lindsey forced a smile after Addie's touching story. "Brian still plays? That's great. He's always been an amazing musician."

"I never knew how much I could enjoy music until Brian stepped in and offered to teach me. Declan, music, and God were the things I was missing while I was trapped in that apartment. I just had to come here to find them."

Lindsey wrung her hands in her lap. "I'm so sorry you had to go through that awful time." Her throat constricted with the pain in Addie's story. "I'm glad you're free now, for all those things you were missing in your life and more."

Now that she thought about the cost of what she gave up when she chose herself over Dakota, the price was too much to bear. Lindsey was missing God too, and the loss felt like a knife in her middle. She'd turned her back on her boyfriend, her friends, this town, and God.

How could she have fallen so far from the person she'd once been? Her attraction to the things of this world had taken her away from the love of her life, as well as her Heavenly Father. Shame covered her in darkness as the emptiness in her chest longed for that connection she'd once felt with her Savior.

Lindsey sighed and looked to Addie. "What if I know now that I was wrong?" she whispered. "I wonder every day if I should've stayed with Dakota. I'll never know if I could've been happier than I am now. I chased that dream into a gutter, and now it doesn't hold any of the glamour that it once did."

She paused to swallow the lump in her throat. "I could've had a completely different life if I'd chosen to stay. Even at the time, I didn't know if I was making the right decision. How do you even know?" Her mind was reeling with what ifs and maybes.

"When it's right, you know."

She looked up at Addie to find her gaze locked on Declan across the room. Lindsey didn't know when they had returned, but Dakota sat beside him, eyes trained on her. She couldn't tell if he wanted to run to her or run through her.

Addie was right about knowing, but Lindsey had known all those years ago and still chose to leave.

Maybe it would be different if the dream she chose had worked out better, but sitting in this room with the people who formed her past, she knew she would have lived those years happier had she stayed here.

Addie gripped her hand as Tyler burst into the room with a beaming smile on his face. "She's here! Sissy is great, and Lydia is perfect." Everyone stood in unison and began hugging and sharing congratulations and well wishes.

The room was buzzing with infectious happiness, and Lindsey was swept into the whirlpool of happy faces around her, thankful to be saved from the spiral her thoughts had been taking.

CHAPTER 5
Dakota

Dakota's thoughts were churning with questions about Lindsey. He was certain she was the one who almost ran him over this morning.

He couldn't help but wonder if she'd purposely tried to kill him. His feelings about her ranged from sadness to happiness to anger but never hit the point of bodily harm. However, he couldn't speak for her.

A pang of longing hit him square in the chest. He certainly couldn't read her mind. Not anymore. At one point in time, he believed he could, but he'd been staring at her with all the concentration he could muster for the last five minutes with no luck. She was still an enigma.

His friend, Declan, had drawn him away from her with the best intentions. Declan knew the hold Lindsey had on him better than anyone, but he also knew exactly how dangerous that kind of connection could be if left unchecked.

Dakota spent years spiraling toward rock bottom after Lindsey left, and Declan had been the one to pick up the pieces. His friend had been stationed in Texas with the U.S. Army at the time, but Declan made every effort to steady his rages from afar. The Army training had been ingrained in Declan's makeup since birth, and the brotherhood he and his friends shared existed long before Declan joined the Army.

He knew Declan had mixed feelings about Lindsey now. They'd been inseparable during high school, but Declan had joined the Army before Lindsey left. Before the breakup. Before he almost threw his life away.

Declan hadn't struggled with his loyalties for long. He was Lindsey's friend, but she made her decision, and Dakota and their shared friends had no choice but to accept it. His friend had witnessed Dakota's downfall, and he could see the blame in Declan's eye now.

"It wasn't her fault." Dakota knew he needed to take responsibility for his part in the mess that ensued after she left.

Declan didn't respond. Of course, he knew it wasn't all her fault, but Dakota needed his friend to know that he understood it too.

"I'm a grown man, and I take full responsibility for what I did. I was stupid, and I deserved what I got. I know you're the most loyal friend on the planet, but you can stop looking at her like you're confused."

Dakota's voice was deadpan, but it carried the honesty he felt.

He was ready to face his part in this, but his heart still hurt. The woman he gave his heart to fully and completely at a young age rejected him, and accepting it was like climbing out of a dark well.

He could hear the empathy in Declan's reply. "I know, man, but that doesn't mean I'm not worried about what could happen while she's here. You went through some pretty dark times after her, and now the biggest hurt in your past is sitting twenty feet away. Forgive me if I would rather you two not end up fighting like two cats trapped in a sack."

"Nothing is going to happen. We're here for Sissy and the baby. Let's just focus on that." Dakota leaned back in the faded brown waiting room chair, crossing his arms over his chest and stretching his legs out to cross them at his ankles.

Dakota didn't have any urge to fight with Lindsey. His anger had dissipated over the years, but his desire for her hadn't. He still wanted her, still loved her, and that was the part that kicked him in the gut every day.

Declan didn't waste any time taking advantage of the change in subject. "Can you believe Sissy is having a baby? Everything is changing so fast."

Dakota huffed a laugh. "Sissy may be younger than all of us, but she's the only one who is ready for a baby."

It was the truth. Sissy was going to be an amazing mother. His sister would take after their own mother in that regard. Children were the force their lives revolved around, and they accepted the nurturing role with pleasure. Plus, Tyler was going to be a great father. It amazed him how much a child could be loved before she was even born.

When Declan didn't respond, he looked up to find his friend staring at Adeline, who looked to be deep in conversation with Lindsey. For the first time, Dakota felt like he didn't know everything going on in his friend's head.

Declan took a deep breath before responding. "I don't know anymore. Addie is different. I know she's the one. For the first time in my life, I know for certain I want kids... with her."

"Dude, don't you think you're moving a little fast? You've only known her for a few months." Dakota tried to keep the accusation out of his voice.

"You of all people should know what it feels like to be sure about the one you want to spend your life with." Declan's response cut like a blade.

"Fair enough, but why rush it?" Dakota asked.

"We're not rushing it. I'll wait a while before asking her to marry me, but we both know it's coming. I would marry her tomorrow, but she deserves time to make sure she wants a life with me."

Dakota could see what the thought of losing Addie did to Declan, and he knew that pain like an old friend. He'd lived with it for years.

"Hey, I've seen you and Addie together these last few months. I don't think she would choose a life without you. I know about loss, and I wouldn't wish that on anyone. Give her the benefit of the doubt." Dakota slapped a hand on his friend's back in an attempt to lighten the mood before dragging his stare back to Lindsey.

He really had no right to give his friend hope about something he'd seen go so terribly wrong himself. He knew the happiness that anyone felt in a relationship could be taken away in an instant. It was all subject to the whims of someone else. Someone you couldn't control. Someone you couldn't force to stay or choose you simply because your life was incomplete and insignificant without her in it.

Dakota's phone buzzed in his pocket, and he checked the text. *Not this again.* He heaved a sigh before replacing the phone in his pocket without responding.

Declan sighed. "I invited my dad over for lunch on Saturday." The confession felt like whiplash in the conversation, but Dakota knew how it fit perfectly. Declan's dad abandoned him and his mother before she died, and Dakota knew his friend hadn't given his dad a second thought after what he did.

"Are you serious? Are you sure he deserves another chance?" Dakota questioned.

"Yes, I'm serious. No, I definitely don't think he deserves a chance. But if I don't start now, my kids may never know their only grandparent." Declan's admission hung in the air for a long minute. Declan's mother and Addie's parents were gone. Their kids wouldn't know the wonderful grandparents they could've had.

"You're a better man than I am. I wouldn't give that low-life two minutes of my time, much less lunch." He stopped to compose himself. "But I see your goal, and it's a good one. Maybe grandkids would give him some motivation to be less of a loser."

Declan smiled at him. "I knew you'd understand. Plus, I think the mending is going to be a long process, so I better start soon."

Dakota's heart beat double time as Tyler came back into the waiting room to tell them Sissy was finally ready for a few visitors.

Tyler addressed the congregation in the waiting room. The sleeves of his button-up shirt were rolled up to the elbows, and he wondered what kind of a panic Tyler had experienced during the delivery.

"She wants to see a few people at a time. She's tired, but we really do want everyone to be able to see Lydia. You've all been patiently waiting, so we'll take a few guests at a time until they need more rest." Tyler was all business, and he wondered again how his sister had found the perfect advocate.

"She asked for Barbara, Lindsey, and Dakota first."

The breath left Dakota's lungs when he heard his name and Lindsey's in the same sentence. Of course she would ask for her mom, best friend, and only sibling first, but the idea of being in such close quarters with Lindsey paralyzed him.

His mother and Lindsey stood in unison and

clasped hands as they made their way for the door. He found the strength to stand and followed them down the yellow-tinged hospital hallway.

His mother slowed her steps and reached for his hand as they walked. "I'm so happy I could burst."

She halted her steps and rested her face in her hands to hide the tears that sprung from her eyes in an instant. He hugged his mother to him with all the strength he could exercise without breaking her and let her cry. He rubbed her back as his own throat constricted. He would never cry, but he was secretly proud of his sister and felt honored to be a new uncle to a healthy baby girl.

"You're going to be the best grandma. Lydia is lucky." He hugged her closer. "We're all lucky to have you, Ma." He kissed the top of her head as she pulled away and wiped her face of tears.

"I always thought you would give me grandkids first." His mom glanced down the hall ahead of them at Lindsey, who had stopped at the door to Sissy's room to wait for them.

"Don't, Ma. I can't get into that right now." His throat tightened as if he was being choked. The life was being pulled from him, and he wanted to run far and fast from this conversation.

"I know. I just hoped all those years ago that it would happen. I just knew it would happen. When it all fell apart, I prayed for the two of you to find the happiness you both deserved. I thought I was going to lose you, Kota." She was crying again, and he felt that familiar guilt for the pain he caused the ones who loved him.

"I'm sorry. I wanted it to work too, but it just can't." He begged her to let it go.

"I understand. I just never worry about Sissy, and I always worry about you. I need both of my babies happy." She stroked his cheek and let her hand fall before grasping his arm and guiding him to Sissy's door.

Lindsey held the door open for Barbara, who patted her arm as she passed into the room. He stopped at the door, waiting for Lindsey to enter.

"Family first," she said, and they made lasting eye contact for the first time.

She was still so beautiful. Her hair was longer than he'd ever seen it, and her natural color was foreign. It reminded him of the color of pine bark. She started dyeing her hair blonde before high school, and the shock of the new color was fading into something that made him feel oddly comfortable. The color and style suited her in an innocent way and matched her warm brown eyes.

He saw the moment she noticed the scar that bisected his eyebrow and wished it didn't exist. He wished that memory was nothing but a dream.

It was like being punched in the gut. The air left his lungs and he was dying... again. She always made him feel things that were above and beyond normal emotions. Now he knew this one for what it was: recognition of mortality.

He couldn't utter a sound as he entered the room ahead of her. His head throbbed with the influx of confusion.

When his eyes landed on Sissy holding the tiny baby, his chest constricted.

How could she be so small? The train of his thoughts shifted, and nothing in the world mattered except the beautiful baby in his sister's arms. His mother cooed at the baby as she peppered kisses on his sister's face, and he could hear Lindsey's sniffles behind him. He stood still as a statue, daring the understanding of such a miracle to come to him.

Sissy turned to him and reached for his hand. She didn't even look tired. The only telling sign of the strain of the day was the redness that lingered in her eyes from crying. "Come meet Lydia. She's amazing." His sister was right. Amazing was an understatement.

He took a tentative step toward the mother and child full of pride and joy. "Sissy, this is incredible." He looked at the puffy red baby face and lost all ability to think.

Sissy handed the tiny bundle to their mother, who accepted it with a smile on her tearstained face. He sat on the hospital bed beside his sister without taking his eyes from the baby. Sissy gripped his hand, and he turned to her.

"I'm so proud of you, Sis. You all right?" Dakota was brimming with happiness for his sister and her family.

"I was *sure* I was dying until they gave me the

meds. After that, I felt like I could fly." She giggled. "No complications, and now I'm on cloud nine with my little Lydia Jane."

"How did Tyler manage?" he asked, but he felt like he already knew the answer. They always gave Tyler a hard time for being such a worrier.

"He was a wreck, as usual. A nurse had to tend to him at one point. He almost passed out." Sissy loved her husband with a fury he'd rarely seen before, but she wasn't above picking at him for being uptight.

"You're kidding! He's a doctor. It's not like he hasn't seen this before," Dakota teased.

Sissy shrugged her shoulders. "He said it's different with someone you love," she defended with a smile.

Their mother stood before him cradling the baby. "Do you want to hold her?"

He wasn't sure if he wanted to hold her or not. Did he even know how to hold a baby? What if he messed her up or broke her? Could that happen?

Sissy saw the indecision and said, "You'll do fine. It's not rocket science. Just hold her like Mom is doing."

Before he could protest, the baby was placed in his arms, and he fidgeted to find a comfortable hold. She was so light and small. This was different from any other first meeting, and he knew as he looked at Lydia's sleeping face that he loved her. Love at first sight most certainly did exist.

"I don't know how you did it, Sis, but she's perfect," he said with pride.

He and Lydia faded into their own world as the women shared the details of the birth. In the quiet that they created for themselves, he wanted to share the happiness he felt. He wanted everyone to know the love he felt in this moment.

A shadow moved in front of him, and he looked up to find Lindsey's solemn face.

"Would you mind if I held her for just a minute?" she asked softly as if she were preparing herself for a refusal.

His heart and mind warred in feeling. The love he was sharing with Lydia today brought back memories of the woman standing before him, the woman he'd loved with all his heart for years. He instinctively pulled the baby tighter to his body in an effort to protect the feeling. He'd been given a taste of happiness again, and he didn't want to lose it this time.

Lindsey shrank in front of him. She'd always been small-framed, but she seemed thinner than he remembered. For all the pain she caused him, why was he still worried about her?

He looked at the baby and felt ridiculous for feeling so territorial of his new niece. He gently passed the baby to Lindsey, and his heart sank at the emptiness he felt when she was gone.

He watched Lindsey's face come alive as she held Lydia, and it tore his insides apart. He'd always been drawn to her, so sure that she was the woman for him. Now, his instincts were screaming as he watched her holding a newborn baby. His heart celebrated at the sight, but his mind was quick to remind him of the false reality before him. The woman he loved would never hold his child like that, and she would never look at him the way he looked at her now.

He'd suffered through this for long enough. He patted Sissy's hand as he stood and made his way for the door fighting anger, guilt, and confusion. He wished there was a way to numb this feeling...

He shut the door behind him and leaned his back against it. He knew better than to let his mind wander that way. Nothing could numb this pain. He knew from experience that drowning his sorrows didn't work. The pain always found a way to swim. He should've learned by now that what's inside the bottle couldn't save him.

Pushing off the door and stalking down the hall, he gave in to his new mission. Maybe he knew better than to chase the numbness, but when had that ever been a good enough reason not to try?

CHAPTER 6

Lindsey

Lindsey spent the next two days attending to her friend and the new baby. It was remarkably easy for her to admit how lovestruck she was by baby Lydia. Normally, Lindsey would've given the new family space and time to themselves, but Sissy insisted she wanted her friend by her side. She knew Sissy well enough to understand the hidden fear behind her request. Lindsey could only imagine how difficult being a new mother must be.

She took shifts with Tyler and Barbara as they all needed time to sleep. When she stayed at the hospital, she tried to be as helpful as possible. Her goal was to stay close enough to be near when Sissy needed her, but far enough away that she didn't interfere with family bonding time.

Lindsey also served as a buffer between the visitors and her friend. She was surprised how many people would try to visit late at night or early in the morning.

Sometimes, Sissy asked her to get rid of them, and she took her job seriously.

After two days of listening intently to the doctors, nurses, Sissy, and Barbara on all things baby related, she felt a foreign sense of comfort in taking care of baby Lydia. The idea of helping to care for a baby was scary and alien to her at first, but she had quickly brushed those reservations away as her fear of the unknown faded.

Lydia was easy to bond with. Lindsey felt uninhibited happiness in her presence and looked forward to every visit. Sissy and Tyler were elated, and she shared their joy. Lindsey watched the family blossom and wondered if she would ever have a time in her life akin to this one.

She'd always wanted a family in her future, but she hadn't been able to give shape to the phantom dream since leaving Carson. Her life had been a bustling fury the past few years, and there wasn't any time to fantasize of a husband and children. Her immediate dreams had burned far too bright to see that distant, domestic future.

Tyler or Barbara had dropped her off at Sissy's house to get some rest a few times before the release from the hospital, and her moments alone were the toughest. Silence always greeted her when she entered her friend's beautiful home. The quiet, empty rooms always fostered thoughts of dread and guilt. She knew the home would soon be filled with cries and laughter when the baby came home, but for now it was an empty tomb.

Dakota hadn't been to the hospital since the day Lydia was born. She didn't have to ask if he'd dropped by, since Sissy continued to question his absence. A few of Dakota's friends stopped by to visit and they each explained that Dakota was having a hard time, but he would manage. They all assured Sissy they would watch out for him, and Lindsey always felt like something wasn't being said in front of her. She felt like part of the conversation was missing or understood to everyone except her.

She shared Sissy's worry over Dakota's absence. He seemed truly happy to see baby Lydia and his sister on that first day, until Lindsey had asked him if she could hold Lydia. He'd flinched and practically ran from the room. She'd pushed him away from his family when they needed him most.

It wasn't uncommon for her to lie in the comfortable guest bed for hours before sleep found her. Exhaustion eventually won her over, and the worry was forced to take a back seat for a while. When she woke, the excitement to get back to her friend's side masked the former worries for a while.

When Sissy and Lydia were discharged at the end of the second day, she could tell Sissy's worry over Dakota had hit a new high. Lindsey continually pulled her friend's attention from Dakota's absence, but sometimes Sissy wouldn't allow herself to be deterred. Even Tyler had attempted to reassure his wife that he'd spoken to Dakota and a few of their friends who were with him. The worry was eating at her, and she would only be placated for brief moments now.

Once the family was safely home, Lindsey excused herself, explaining that she needed to run into town for a few things. She couldn't let Sissy sit around worried for her brother when she should be celebrating the new addition to her family.

She didn't know where to begin looking for him. It had been years since she really knew him, but it couldn't hurt to start with some of the places he used to hang out.

She couldn't believe Dakota wasn't visiting his family because he was still upset with her. How could he be so selfish and cause so much worry because of the problems between them? As she drove, her temper only grew, and she stopped giving him the benefit of the doubt.

She quickly realized she didn't even know what type of vehicle he drove anymore, so she couldn't just drive by the places she thought she might possibly find him. She drove, parked, and scanned every establishment in town where he would possibly frequent.

After two hours of hunting, she was running out of possible hang outs for him. She'd driven to the outskirts of town when she had an idea, and it wasn't one that boded well for her.

What if he wasn't in town? What if he was at home, or the place he used to call home?

Dakota's family owned a large expanse of land

outside the town limits. The house he and Sissy grew up in was a striking white plantation style home surrounded by trees and endless grassy hills, but that wasn't the home she thought of now.

Dakota's home was the place of refuge he partitioned for himself long ago on the edge of the reaching acres of his family land. The rolling hills of the meadow were surrounded by forests where they used to explore and search for sticks to fuel the fires they congregated around on cool autumn nights in their high school days. A pond sat nestled at the entrance of the field where they used to fish for bass in Dakota's father's canoe, and the old, wooden barn that Dakota and his friends had commandeered as their refuge sat nestled on a small rise a hundred feet from the bank of the pond.

Her heart hammered as she thought of the place while she drove. She knew it like her own childhood home. The one she'd loved and then missed when she and then her parents left Carson and her childhood behind. It was the land she grew up on, the hills that had heard her laughter, the soil that had soaked up her tears.

Back when life was full of hopes and dreams of their future together, she and Dakota spent endless hours brainstorming the house they planned to build when they were finally married. She and Sissy had peppered Dakota with design ideas, and he'd pretended to listen with a smirk on his face.

She was fully capable of understanding Dakota's

attachment to the place because she felt it too. Sometimes, she still wondered why she'd ever wanted to be anywhere but here. Dakota dug his boots into this dirt, and any talk of moving had been futile. He was meant to grow old here, and she knew it too.

The Calhoun family had lived on the same land they loved, as far back as any of them knew. The land was a part of them, and even Sissy appreciated its weight in their family. They were lucky enough to live in a gift of nature, and Dakota shared his love with his friends.

Dakota's dad died of a heart attack when he was only twelve and Sissy nine. She remembered the little boy who didn't understand his grief, and she knew the place he always ran to as his haven. He let Sissy join him there on the few occasions when she sought him out, but overall the place was claimed by Dakota when his world fell apart. When he finally began to let people in again, his friends helped him through his grief in the place where he felt most comfortable.

Beginning in middle school, their group of friends took full advantage of the land and its endless possibilities for adventure. They scoured every inch of it and left no stone unturned. She was sure that somewhere there existed printed photos developed from disposable cameras that memorialized those golden days.

When they entered high school, things didn't change all that much, except that their parents didn't make them come in before dark. She spent every weekend at Dakota's with their friends. They all made for the barn as soon as school let out, sometimes forgetting that Monday morning did actually exist in the world they immersed themselves in.

Dakota and their friends took charge of the old barn on the property when they were fourteen. They spent the summer patching up broken boards and reinforcing beams and ladders.

The idea was to make a permanent place to sleep indoors so they could stop building tents every weekend. The girls had always made their way home soon after nightfall, but the boys were content to sleep outdoors if the weather permitted.

They lined one whole wall of the barn with bunks and sleeping nooks. Each of their friends partitioned out his own place and claimed it to do with as he pleased. She and Sissy bribed their friend, Brian, into building them their own bunk and space in the barn.

Driving toward her past felt like a dream. There were too many memories, too much love, and not enough remorse. She sure had a way of sabotaging anything good in her life.

Dakota was the love of her life, and she swallowed the lump in her throat at the realization. She would always love him, whether they ended up together in the end or not.

Her heart constricted as she neared the property. How had she been so blind? How could she have ever thought he would choose her over this place? Granted, she hadn't given him that ultimatum. She'd been too afraid of his answer, but now she understood the worth of such a place.

Now, Lindsey didn't know where home was anymore. She was better off forgotten in the place she wished she could call home. This place felt like the only home that would always call to her.

Dakota loved this place, and it was one thing he would always fight to keep. This was the one thing that would never leave him... unlike her.

She wiped a stray tear from her face and remembered her mission. Find Dakota. Convince him to at least call Sissy to ease her mind.

This visit was for Sissy, and she would do anything for her friend. Even if it meant facing the one man who hated her.

CHAPTER 7
Lindsey

The clouds hung low over the field, sending menacing shadows into her path as she drove her old junker over the dam that ran along one side of the pond. The midday sun was shielded by the dark sky, and she said a small prayer that the rain would hold off.

When the clearing in front of the barn came into view, she noticed a fire was burning in the pit they'd always used, and three men casually stood around the flames. They turned to look at her as she neared, and the closest one even took a step toward her. He probably assumed she was lost.

She recognized her old friend Marcus approaching her car as she parked beside the barn in the same spot she'd once claimed for herself years ago. Back then, her car was parked here so often that the grass refused to grow. The grass was naturally reclaimed now, and it made her heart sick for what had once been.

It was a wonder she even recognized Marcus now. If she hadn't spent years of her life with him as friends, she wouldn't be able to perceive the noticeable way he walked. His dark hair was longer than he kept it before and shaggy in an I-don't-care sort of way that accentuated his signature bad boy look. He was bigger now, and she had to remind herself that she hadn't laid eyes on him in six years. Of course, he was a man now. Thick cords of muscle covered his arms, and she turned away from him to face the dim midday sun.

If she didn't know Marcus, she would've been terrified of him. His face had never been blatantly friendly, but she once knew him for the caring friend he was. She could see past his hard exterior to the man he hid from the world. She knew his past, his heartaches, his losses, but she had to remind herself that she really didn't know him at all anymore.

His progress toward her came to a halt when she stepped from the car and faced him. Surely, he knew she was in town, but he looked taken aback when he noticed who stood before him.

The moment of shock was gone as fast as it had arrived, and he simply said, "You shouldn't be here."

His words were direct and true, but they went against her mission. If no one else would talk sense into Dakota, she would have to do it herself.

"I'm looking for Dakota. Have you seen him?" She wouldn't back down.

Marcus looked back to the two men remaining at

the fire, and she noticed one was Declan and the other was Ian, another of her old friends.

"I don't think you have any right to know where he is," Ian said. "If he wanted to talk to you, I guess he'd have done it already."

She and Ian butted heads a few times over the years, but they'd never meant to inflict lasting harm. Now, she got the feeling he wished his words were knives.

"It's not about me. It's for Sissy," she defended herself.

"Is she all right?" Declan asked.

"She's just about worried sick, and she won't be pacified until Dakota shows his face. She just wants to know he's all right." Lindsey prayed they would understand.

"He'll be fine. Forgive him if he's a little under the weather right now," Ian barked sarcastically at her as he threw his empty soda can into the trash bin with a bit too much force. His stare never left her.

Declan turned to Ian and said, "Maybe we should let her have a try. You know we're not making much progress with him, and I'm tired of treating him like a child. She started this, so maybe she should fix it."

Now she was getting somewhere.

"What do you mean 'she started this'?"

The men ignored her and continued arguing.

"Oh, you think *she* is the answer?" Ian spat the word *she* like it was a curse. Like he couldn't bear to speak her name.

"I don't feel like fighting Dakota's battles for him anymore today," Marcus said with finality. He turned to her, but his eyes weren't looking at her; they were seeing into her heart. Searching her intentions. "He's on the ridge in the west corner of the field." He pointed to the edge of the field over the hills and out of sight. "Be warned. He had a handle of Jack when he stormed off, and that was an hour ago."

Jack? Since when did Dakota drink anything but cheap beer and only on the weekends?

Sometime since she stopped knowing anything about him, apparently.

"Thanks, guys." She got back into her car and followed the tire tracks through the tall grass that led in the direction Marcus indicated.

She found Dakota at the tree line that surrounded the property. He was carrying the bottle of Jack Daniels in one hand and lining up empty beer cans on the fence posts. She was sure he could hear her car approaching, but he hadn't even spared a glance her way yet.

Stealing a second for herself, she took a deep breath as she gave herself a pep talk for this conversation.

The wind whipped her long, straight hair in a whirlwind around her as she stepped from the car. The empty can he'd just placed blew from its throne atop the fence post and his curse was carried to her on the waves of the breeze. Lindsey hugged her arms around herself, despite the unseasonably warm October air.

She was about five feet away from him when he

turned to her for a split second before giving his attention back to his task of placing cans.

"Are you here to finish what you started?" His words were sharp, but they were also hollow.

Her chest constricted, but she found the courage to ask, "What do you mean?"

"I assume you meant to put me out of my misery when you almost ran me over." He stalked past her and picked up a rock from a pile in the grass.

She didn't speak, just watched him walk past her without any of the care he once showed for her.

"I think I'm about tired of this." He threw the half empty bottle of whiskey into the field and threw the rock at one of the cans lined on the fence posts, missing by a foot to the right.

"What does that tell you, Lindsey?" His words had dropped to a whisper full of shame, and he wouldn't look at her.

Terror and confusion gripped her. Dakota was strong. He never gave up, always finished anything he started, and he never let his determination falter. "I don't know, Dakota, but you've been drinking, and..."

She was scrambling her words because her heart was breaking. His words were tearing her apart. Her chest ached, and she couldn't breathe. "Dakota, please don't say things like that."

She barely finished the last word before he spat back at her, "Why not? Huh? Give me a reason, Lindsey."

"Lydia," she paused. "Sissy, your mom, Declan, Marcus, Ian, Brian, Jake." She was pulling names of friends she hadn't laid eyes on in years, but maybe they still meant something. She named the people who had once meant the world to him.

He pointed his finger at her face and growled, "You know the one name I want on that list more than anything is missing." Dakota linked his fingers around the back of his neck and turned his back on her. His black hair blew softly in the wind, and she could smell the rain coming. The air was thick with moisture around them.

He took a few slow steps before rounding on her with renewed fury. His eyes were blazing and bloodshot from drinking.

"She's gone!" he yelled, throwing his hands out, gesturing to the emptiness around him.

He was raving mad, and she had no idea how to help him. She hadn't talked him off a ledge like this in all the years she'd known him.

The man in front of her wasn't the boy she knew.

She grasped for the one thing she hoped would penetrate his drunken haze. "Sissy needs you, Dakota. She's worried about you."

"I can't go to her like this. She'll hate me. I can't lose her too." He said it like she should know better. "I almost lost her once, and now I've made the same mistake again. I'm meant to sabotage anything good in my life."

"I don't know what you're talking about, but..."

He'd taken the two steps that lay between them in long, quick strides before she could finish her sentence. Grabbing her shoulders hard, he shook her, forcing her to look at him.

"Why wasn't I enough? I have to know. I would've done anything for you. I would've given you anything. I wanted you to do all the things you wanted, and all I asked was to be able to stand beside you through everything." His words were quick and frantic as he shook her.

She stared at him dumbfounded. "Dakota. I can't. I... I'm sorry. It's just..." What was she supposed to say? She wanted to say so much, but the words wouldn't come out.

His mouth found hers in the instant of her hesitation, and she forgot anything she was trying to say. His arms pulled her in tight as his mouth laid claim to hers. He pressed their bodies tighter and her hands involuntarily wrapped around him, seeking a closeness that seemed so near, yet so far.

She didn't care about anything but this feeling and the man holding her. The man she loved and cherished. This was where she was meant to be. That home she'd been searching for felt so close, and she didn't want to let it go.

The embers that kindled easily turned into a fire. Raging, engulfing, unstoppable.

He broke the kiss and whispered against her ear, "I missed you," as if the words would scare her away.

"I missed you too," she replied in a daze.

"I always dream about you. About us."

Tears filled her eyes, and she swallowed to push them back. She wanted to hold him like this and never let go. Neither of them moved, afraid to break the connection for fear of the fall from the mountain they were perched on. They were paralyzed for long minutes before he braced one arm on the truck and pulled his face away to look at her.

She willed the tears to stop. Wished they hadn't come. She felt vulnerable and scared of anything that came next because it was bound to hurt. The fall from the top of the mountain was painful, and once vivid colors seemed pale in comparison.

Sometimes she wished she was blissfully ignorant to the emotions he made her feel.

He tensed beside her, and her breathing stopped. Lindsey's chest constricted, and she couldn't bear to turn to him. She could feel it radiating from him, and when she did look, she saw it written on his face.

Disgust.

He was drunk, and he had no idea what he'd said or done.

The shame washed over her and congregated in her throat. How could she have been so careless? She'd let him use her simply because she'd been hypnotized by the illusion of something she felt in the moment.

And now the moment was gone, and she felt like dirt. No, she felt like the dirt on the bottom of a shoe. She was being continually trampled on, and she had allowed it. She'd done nothing to save her dignity, and now it was gone with the wind.

She couldn't look at him, and she certainly didn't want him to see her tears. Turning to hide her face from him, her gaze landed on a tattoo that stretched across the forearm he braced against the truck, and she tilted her head to read it.

The word Bonnie, written in gothic font, took up most of the inside of his forearm.

As the realization hit her, he pulled his arm away and quickly stepped back. He was scrambling away from her now, but she wasn't going to let him get away that easy.

"You have a tattoo that says Bonnie? When did you get that?" She stood her ground and questioned him. "I thought you were against tattoos. You said they were a waste of the money you worked so hard for."

"Don't worry about it. It's nothing. Just a..." He turned away from her and bent to grab another beer corpse from the ground.

"I'm pretty sure it's something, *Clyde*." She threw the nickname at him for the first time in years, and he flinched like he'd been struck.

"So, there was another Bonnie in your life after me?"

"No," he practically yelled at her. "It was you, but it was too late." He threw the can into the back of his truck.

Lindsey stood there waiting for answers. She was the Bonnie to his Clyde, and it had been them against the world. Their friends gave them the nicknames after a scandalous run-in with the law when they were young.

"When?" was all she asked.

"It doesn't matter!"

"It matters to me," she was yelling back now, and she was glad they were so far away from civilization.

"Leave. Go. Now." He threw the words at her and left no room to argue, but she wasn't finished.

"Dakota…"

"If you don't leave, I will. You ran me out of New York, and now you're running me off my own land. Why can't you just let me have the things I love?" He was screaming, pleading with her now.

She felt sick. She was going to be sick right here, right now.

"I'll go," she whispered. Dakota only stared at her, his chest heaving in anger.

When she reached her car, he hadn't moved a muscle. Turning to him, she pleaded, "Please go see Sissy. She needs to know you're okay. She loves you…"

He turned away from her before she finished speaking, and she felt his absence like a hole in her middle.

Lindsey sat in her car and cried. Her frustration, love, and hurt bubbled to the surface and refused to let her leave unchanged. Dakota was wrestling with his own problems, and she'd been too caught up in herself to notice.

Ian's words from earlier struck her heart. This *was* her fault.

What was worse? She didn't know how to help him this time.

Lindsey drove away from him and wondered how she would ever fix the mess that lay between them.

CHAPTER 8
Dakota

The pain was born of nothing. It came into existence in an unsuspecting moment and gripped his head in a vice. He willed it to leave, begged it to recede, but it was useless. He was waking up to a hangover, and he deserved it.

Dakota's head was pounding from the alcohol assault yesterday, but the ache in his chest rivaled the stabbing in his head. Missing her almost felt worse than the hangover, and his shame wasn't far behind.

When Lindsey showed up yesterday, he was half gone and ready to give in to the anger she kindled in him. He'd been ready to rage, scream, and throw things.

But he'd kissed her instead.

Why did he do it? That was a rhetorical question. How could he forget? He'd heard the rejection coming and decided he couldn't bear it again. The answers he hoped and prayed for didn't abide in her, and he wouldn't survive another loss like before. He'd been incredibly lucky to have survived once.

He'd sent her away because he couldn't love her openly anymore, and he couldn't trust her to stay. She would leave, and he would be left here like before. She wasn't staying, and he couldn't forget that important fact.

Yesterday was a hazy memory, but the moments with her were crystal clear, and he would protect them for eternity. It may be the only thing he would have left to sustain him. Her lips were soft and smooth, her skin was warm and flawless, her brown eyes were striking and captivating. She still took his breath away.

Dakota hated himself for what he did to her, and now she would have one more reason to hate him too.

He slowly moved to a sitting position while clutching his head as it throbbed in protest. He rested his elbows on his knees and crushed his hanging head between his hands, feeling like it might explode any moment.

He felt like a dog with its tail between his legs. A tiny woman could bring him to his knees. She seemed skinnier than before and much smaller than the larger-than-life presence that messed with his mind on a regular basis.

A half empty bottle of whiskey sat on the night stand beside the bed, promising another day that he wouldn't have to face the pain. He grabbed for it, but Lindsey's beautiful voice rang in his mind.

Sissy. Lindsey said Sissy needed him, and he

remembered how much he'd already put his sister through in the last few years. She needed him to pull himself out of this death trap.

He let his hand slip from the bottleneck and rubbed his face furiously. He could do this.

Maybe he could do this, but seeing Lindsey again would send him back spiraling. He knew it. After the way she made him question everything yesterday, he was sure to end up back off the wagon.

Why couldn't he manage life the way other people did? Why did he default to this same toxic crutch? He hated that he was always apologizing and asking for forgiveness.

His neck ached as his head rose, and he spotted the Bible resting on the bedside table. Another day of turning his head in shame. Another day of falling short. How long would he be praying the same prayer of forgiveness? He was tired of needing help and failing in every way that mattered. He almost couldn't be trusted with his own life.

Lindsey didn't need him. He couldn't even be the godly man he promised he would be for her all those years ago. Why would he drag her down with him? He wasn't worthy, and she deserved more.

His phone buzzed on the bedside table, and he hesitated before checking it. Sure enough, it was *her* again. Only a couple of days since her last text. If Tara kept up at this rate, he'd be changing his number again by the end of the month.

He stood slowly and made his way to the kitchen

while supporting himself on sturdy surfaces. Maybe coffee would help, but he needed water at the very least.

His bedroom was a wreck, but at least the rest of the house was decent. He tried not to spend enough time here to harm the place.

He couldn't stand this house. He hated the way it provoked him. The house was useless... all for nothing. It was all wasted on him and his empty dreams.

The silence taunted him here. He had imagined this place completely different, and his expectations killed the reality.

This house was supposed to be a haven, a comfort from any peril the world could throw at him. It was meant for the noises and voices of a family and lives being lived. Now it just seemed like a ridiculous waste of time.

His anger was bubbling again, and his breath came in short pants. The coffee finished brewing, and he grabbed a mug with shaky hands before placing it on the counter beside the steaming carafe. The aroma alone should have warmed him, but right now it smelled muted and stale.

His hand trembled as he lifted the decanter, and he focused his concentration on controlling the spasms to no avail. Not even half of the coffee he poured ended up in the mug, and his surrender was instantaneous. He brought the pot down onto the counter with too much force and glass shattered as coffee spilled around him.

"Really?" He threw the remainder of the decanter into the sink and linked his fingers behind his neck.

He didn't move, just stood there with his eyes closed, breathing through the frustration.

He heard his cell ringing in the bedroom and ignored it in favor of the impromptu meditation he desperately needed in order to hang onto his sanity. If that was her again, he might lose his mind.

A moment of silence came, then the ringing started again. He calmed enough to search for the phone without wishing he could strangle the caller. He grabbed it without checking the caller ID.

"Hello."

"So you live to see another day," Marcus said. His friend wasn't one to coddle, and he knew how short Marcus' patience could be.

"Lucky me."

"That 'poor me' attitude doesn't work on me, brother," Marcus replied.

Dakota spat, "I'm not asking for you to feel sorry for me. I just feel like I've been hit in the head with a baseball bat."

"Well..." Marcus began.

"I know. I brought this on myself. I've heard your rousing pep talks before," Dakota said.

"You should be well rested at least. You passed out around six last night."

Dakota looked at the clock to see it was nine in the morning. "Thanks... for whatever you did for me yesterday. Not gonna say I remember getting in bed," he said.

"I'm done, Dakota. I'm not your babysitter, and you're a grown man. Get your act together. I mean it. Get up because I'm on my way to pick you up. You're going to see Sissy and the baby today," Marcus said.

Marcus had expressed tough love for him before, but he'd never thrown in the towel. Dakota probably should've stopped pushing his friend's limits a long time ago.

"I planned to go see them today anyway."

"Good thing. I wasn't about to give you a choice." Marcus hung up the phone, and Dakota threw it onto the bed and went to get a shower.

Marcus pulled into the roundabout in front of Tyler and Sissy's house and threw the car in park.

"Get out," Marcus said, stern but even. He never yelled, but he had a way of making himself heard without volume.

"I haven't fought this, have I?" Dakota felt the need to defend himself. Sure, his friend was angry with reason, but he hadn't been difficult this morning.

Marcus sat staring at him, waiting on his exit.

"Aren't you coming in?" Dakota asked.

"No. I was here this morning when Sissy was in tears worried about you. So, no. I'm not coming in. It's your turn, and you better make it good. Do whatever you have to do to convince her you're perfectly fine."

Well, that was harsh. "I *am* fine." Once again, Dakota was defending himself and still wondering why he bothered.

"Listen, I've got everything under control. You don't need to babysit me anymore. I'm fine." He was still trying to convince himself, but he was closer to fine than he'd been when the light pierced his eyes first thing this morning.

"Get out." He could tell Marcus was fed up with him, so he got out of his friend's precious sports car without another word.

Marcus sped off before Dakota even reached the door, and he felt all the shame that had been accumulating in the back of his mind the last few days. He remembered this feeling, and he hated it just as much now as before.

The people who still cared if he was ruining his life were scarce these days. Unfortunately, they were the ones he loved the most and hated hurting. He hurt them every time he messed up like he did yesterday, and then the shame showed its ugly head. He was sick of this feeling, and he decided he wouldn't give in to the temptation again. He was determined to face his problems just like everyone else. Even if they came in the sinfully gorgeous package named Lindsey.

The door was unlocked, and he let himself in. The scream stopped him in his tracks, and his hands covered his ears as the wailing paralyzed him.

Coming here with a hangover was a terrible idea.

He forced his eyes to open and found Tyler

striding toward him with a look of determination on his face.

"Get in there now." Tyler grabbed his collar and slung him in the direction of the sitting room to his left. "She's been a mess waiting for you, and the baby is picking up on her foul mood. Get in there and make Lydia go back to sleep."

"Chill out, Ty. I'm here now," Dakota said.

He stumbled into the room to find Sissy pacing in a circle while bouncing Lydia in her arms. His sister's face was pink and stray strands of greasy, black hair had come free of her ponytail.

Guilt punched him in the gut when he heard the song Sissy was singing in an attempt to pacify Lydia. Her words were uneven and labored, but he recognized the lullaby she sang to him once after their dad died. It was a song to comfort with promises that everything would be all right and better days were coming.

Judging from the look on Sissy's face, he would bet money she was singing the song to quiet her own fears.

He took a step toward her and she stopped cold when she turned to him.

"Kota." The one word pierced the room before the sobs took her and she fell to her knees with the baby in her arms. He hadn't noticed Lindsey sitting on the couch until she jumped to her friend's side and whispered to her as she gently took Lydia into her arms.

Lindsey stood with the baby and turned to him. Her beauty stopped his breath. She always affected him this way. Her long, brown hair hung in loose waves over her shoulders and her face was bare. She rarely wore makeup when they were together before, and it was an unwelcome change when she started wearing it in New York. Lindsey was naturally flawless, and the makeup hid some of her beauty.

He was powerless before her, and he hated his lack of control. His pulse quickened with his breaths, and his fingers tingled with the urge to touch her. He would always think of her as his. At least his body would always recognize her as his other half. She should be in his arms right now.

He knew her well enough to read the anger on her face, but he also saw the hidden hurt in her brown eyes. It was all his fault.

"We'll give you two some privacy." Lindsey practically flew out of the room, and it took all his control not to chase her. He wanted her in his arms more than anything. He wanted to feel her warm skin again and taste her sweet lips. He'd forgotten how much he drew strength from the comfort of her presence.

Sissy was still sobbing, although quieter now. He was acutely aware of the silence outside of her whimpers, and it felt wrong.

He crossed to her and bent to help her to her feet. He helped her get seated on the couch, and then pulled a decorative chair from the corner of the room to sit beside her.

"Sissy," he whispered to get her attention.

She sniffled and wiped at her face frantically before

pulling a baby bib from the waistband of her sweatpants and blowing her nose on it.

"She only wakes up for a few hours a day, but those few hours of crying are enough to make me question everything I'm doing." She rubbed the bib across her face again before dropping her hands into her lap and looking to him. "Where have you been?"

Dakota hesitated. He hated the accountability of the next day. "I was drinking, but it's done. I'm fine now, and you don't have to worry another minute. I'm going to talk to Lindsey and get a grip on my problems."

"I'm sorry, Dakota. I knew this would be hard for you, but I... just thought you were past this."

"I am. I am." He grabbed her hand. "I'm sorry. I was weak for a minute. I hate that I worried you. I'm here now, and everything is fine."

He meant every word. Seeing Sissy crumble to the floor had built his resolve. This wasn't Lindsey's fault. It was his. Seeing her shouldn't send him spiraling. It was his own weak mind to blame.

He needed help, but he was too ashamed to ask God for what he needed most.

"You said that last time, and I still almost lost you."

He couldn't blame her for doubting him. He hadn't proven reliable in the past, but things were going to change now. He would have to confront Lindsey and deal with this the right way.

"I know, but I'm working on being better. I'll get there. Promise, Sis."

She stopped crying, and now she looked exhausted. He and Sissy had weathered everything together, but he'd never seen her look so defeated.

"You take a week off work and use it to go off the deep end. So typical." She wiped stray tears from under her eyes, and he relaxed a small fraction. If she was making light of the situation, he knew she was forgiving him.

"I'm going to see if Lindsey needs help with Lydia. Take a nap. You look awful." It was all he had to offer her, and he secretly wanted a chance to see Lindsey. He'd been itching to talk to her since he made up his mind to face her and get things out in the open.

Her eyes glimmered with unshed tears as she ignored his joking insult. "Thank you." She wiped her eyes again. "I swear I'm not going soft. This is a temporary thing. The hormones are extreme."

"You're the strongest woman I know." She was his baby sister, but she'd carried him through all of his dark times. He would never accuse her of being weak.

He squeezed her arm as he stood to leave.

"Kota," Sissy's voice was quiet, but he recognized the attitude he'd been missing. He turned to her and didn't have to fake a smile.

Sissy was grinning too. "Play nice."

CHAPTER 9
Lindsey

Lindsey paced the nursery, bouncing Lydia on her shoulder. The baby fell asleep about five minutes ago, but the walking helped clear her mind.

She thanked God again that Dakota finally showed up. Sissy was ready to pack up and look for him herself, and she and Tyler weren't going to be able to hold her off much longer when Dakota had finally stumbled in the door.

Lindsey still wasn't sure of all the details, but she knew enough to gather that Dakota probably had a drinking problem, but she wondered if he was battling something else.

Depression and alcoholism made the best of friends. She'd seen more ruined performers resort to substance abuse and depression than she'd ever dreamed during her time away from Carson. The entertainment industry either built confidence or destroyed it. She counted herself lucky to have gotten out before things turned ugly for her.

She often thought of her exit from the entertainment industry as cowardice, but every once in a while, she felt like it was a brave move.

When she failed to convince Dakota to make an appearance yesterday, she decided not to mention her failed errand to Sissy. She certainly hadn't felt that telling Sissy what she found would help matters.

Hugging Lydia's sleeping body to her tightly, she continued to pace and wonder how the meeting downstairs was going. Sissy hadn't slept since they came home from the hospital, and she was almost certain Tyler hadn't either.

The door of the quiet nursery creaked, and she turned to find Dakota slipping into the room. His T-shirt was wrinkled, and his hair was wet and tousled. She was still upset with him, but she couldn't deny that he made bedhead look good.

But when she saw his face, her anger from yesterday began to build back up. She remembered how he'd misled her and given her false hope. He'd held her, but the caring feelings from before were missing. The final straw was the not-so-subtle kick in the pants at the end. He didn't care about her, and he didn't want her here.

She would be the first to take responsibility for hurting him all those years ago, but the hurt he inflicted on her yesterday was new and still sore. Her anger felt completely valid.

He noticed the sleeping baby and his movements became inaudible. Dakota was a hunter if she ever saw one, and she suddenly felt like prey. She'd never been scared of him before, but in this moment she felt helpless and unprepared.

A cornered animal never surrenders quietly.

He stopped about a foot away from her and whispered, "Can we talk?"

She wanted to lay Lydia in her crib, but she didn't want to turn her back to him. It was irrational, since he'd never hurt her before—so long as heartache didn't count.

She was having trouble thinking clearly when he was standing so close. He was much larger than she remembered. Dakota had always been broad shouldered and muscular, but now he was bigger and she was even smaller.

Standing her ground fueled by the anger and hurt she felt fresh from yesterday, she resolutely said, "No."

He adjusted his stance and his brows drew together. "Why not?" His voice was tempered and controlled, but she knew it came with a price.

"I don't think it's a good idea." She backed away from him before she knew she was moving, until her back touched the crib. The wooden beams felt like a fence, causing panic to rise in her.

She saw the moment he understood. "Are you afraid of me? Come on, Lindsey, I've never hurt anyone but myself." His voice rose as he continued speaking.

"No. Whatever you're mixed up in is hurting Sissy, and it scares me," she said in a whisper to remind him of the sleeping baby in her arms. "I'm not in the mood to get hurt again."

"*You* aren't in the mood to get hurt? Are you kidding me right now?" His volume rose again, but she met his rage.

"You misled me yesterday—"

He cut her off before she could finish. "I may have been well on my way to being drunk, but I don't remember any objection from you."

Her blood was boiling. She was too angry to speak, and her jaw ached as she ground her teeth together.

Before she could compose herself to retaliate, Tyler entered the room and spat, "Outside. Both of you. Now."

Dakota left the room without looking back, and she turned to place Lydia down in her crib.

When she made her way downstairs, she found Tyler and Dakota in the kitchen. Tyler leaned against the sink staring at Dakota like he was planning his slow death. Dakota was propped against the bar on the other side of the kitchen, arms and ankles crossed, meeting Tyler's fiery gaze match for match.

She saw a small piece of the old Dakota then. She was sure he'd never backed down from anything in his life.

Tyler broke his stare at her entrance and pushed away from the counter. "Whatever you two have going on, fix it now." He pointed a finger that swiveled between Dakota and herself. "Sissy needs both of you right now, and I just need you to stop fighting. Kiss and make up for all I care, but please do something."

She felt the heat rise in her cheeks and hugged her arms around her middle. The last thing she needed was a reminder of the flippant way they'd failed to communicate yesterday.

Tyler jerked his head to Dakota to find him suddenly interested in the grocery list stuck to the refrigerator and threw his hands in the air. "You already did, didn't you? Get out, and don't come back until you've fixed your problems."

Dakota stood up straight. "Wait, I told Sissy I would help with Lydia while she napped."

"I'm here, and Barbara is on her way. I think we have this covered." Tyler ended the argument and left the room without a parting glance at either of them.

"Bye, Ty," Dakota taunted.

The momentary shock of Tyler's outburst wore off and she found her voice. "You want to talk outside?"

"Sure." He didn't look at her as he led the way to the back door and outside. The warm October sun was a shock to her system, after the bouts of screaming and complete silence of the house. The shade of a giant oak tree fell just short of the space where her car was parked.

Dakota hadn't looked at her yet, and that made it easier to speak. He pinched the bridge of his nose and squeezed his eyes shut against the blinding noon sun.

"I can't believe we acted like that," she said timidly, bringing her arms to wrap around her chest.

"Yeah, that was pretty bad. I've never seen Tyler so mad before." Dakota seemed to have moved past his anger as he rubbed his chin and considered Tyler's behavior. "Actually, I've never seen him mad. Ever. And trust me, I've tried to rile him up a few times."

"He hasn't been sleeping much. The baby keeps everyone awake, since they're afraid to take their eyes off her. Being a new parent is tough."

She was reluctant to say anymore, but Tyler had practically ordered them to talk about things. Kicking a stone in the path, she looked down and said, "I've never seen you like I saw you yesterday."

He looked at her like it was the first time he'd laid eyes on her, and she felt the heat of his stare in her bones.

"I had a problem..." he began and looked away.

"Had or have?" she asked.

"I don't know. I'm trying." He wrapped his hands behind his neck and took a deep breath.

"Why do you do it?" She'd been wondering since she saw him yesterday, and she couldn't bring herself to piece it all together with the boy she once knew. That boy she knew was in his early twenties with a steady job and didn't have a care in the world. He worked, made good money, paid his bills, and spent his free time with her and his friends.

How much could have changed?

"I can't handle my demons. They just snuck up on me again this week," he said matter of fact.

"Are you saying this is my fault?" she asked, and her pitch rose with the accusation. It wasn't the first time she'd been blamed for Dakota's problems.

"No, I'm a grown man, and I take full responsibility for my mistakes." He ran his fingers through his hair, accentuating the mess. "You just used to bring out the best in me, and now you seem to call to my faults."

She had to find some way to remind him of the wonderful life he used to have, or maybe help him realize he still had it. "Is there anything left in you of the carefree boy I used to know?" she asked.

His gaze bored into hers with all the fire he used to hold for her, and she knew his answer before he said the words.

"No. He's gone." His words were final, and she felt her heart break for the man she used to love.

Her chest began to ache as she recognized the loss of what they'd been and could never be again. She would do things so differently, if only she could go back. Lindsey may not have been ready to settle down with him all those years ago, but now she knew she could never have that chance back. Things had changed while she was away, and they were different people in the wake of the years between them.

"Listen, I'm sorry for the way I treated you yesterday." His hand rose as if he meant to reach for her but changed direction and he scratched the back of his head. "You don't deserve to be treated that way. Ever. And I understand why you're mad at me. I was a jerk, and I hate myself for it. I want to make it up to you."

He turned to look back at the house they'd just been kicked out of and sighed. "I want to show you that, yeah, I've changed, but I'm not that guy you saw yesterday. That was the worst version of me, and it won't happen again."

She had every reason to believe him, and it was easy to nod her acceptance of his apology. "I believe you."

They'd weathered fights before, but the disagreements were never serious. In all the years they'd dated, he'd never given her a reason to believe he would cheat on her. They'd been too young to argue over finances or other serious issues, and their arguments had been more playful than harmful. He'd never once said or done anything to purposely hurt or upset her, and that had always been the line she thought they would never cross.

"You wanna start slow?" he asked.

She gave a small nod. "I think we can do that."

"How about lunch at The Line? I know you're a big city girl now, but maybe you can slum it for one meal." He winked and butterflies jumped in her middle, bringing back memories of that casual gesture and what it did to her.

She realized that maybe Sissy hadn't kept him updated about the goings-on in her life after she left. She hadn't asked Sissy about Dakota even once for fear it would make missing him unbearable. Perhaps it was only fair that her friend kept quiet on both ends.

What if he hadn't ever asked about her? What would that mean? Maybe his reasons were the same as hers, but it would kill another piece of her heart if he hadn't asked about her because he simply hadn't cared.

Lindsey hadn't been to the city in years, and he apparently didn't know about that little detail. She'd lived in a few different places since then, but she knew what he meant when he mentioned the big city. That city could only be New York City where her journey started.

The fire died out in her. She didn't know why, but she felt lighter. The anger in her subsided for now, and she wanted to take advantage of this moment of peace. The Line was their place, and she knew he suggested it as a way to make her feel comfortable.

"Sure." The lone word felt inadequate, considering the circumstances.

"Can I bum a ride? Marcus dropped me off earlier."

"Sure, but why did Marcus bring you?" They walked to her car casually, as if they hadn't just hashed it out inside the house.

He opened the driver's side door for her and admitted, "I may have not known what day it was this morning when he came by to check on me."

CHAPTER 10
Dakota

Dakota kept reminding himself not to stare at her as she drove along the winding county road toward The Line, but it was a test of strength not to watch her.

Her chestnut hair danced in the wind, as free as she'd always been. Lindsey was a carefree creature who always stopped to enjoy the beauty in the world around her. He couldn't blame the wind for wrapping her in its warm breeze. She was most at home with her eyes closed and her head tilted to welcome the sun.

Lindsey drove with her arm propped on the open window and an easy grin on her face. Shadows from the leafy canopy that covered the lonely backroad skimmed her face, creating new and exciting contrasts to enjoy. He'd missed seeing her for too long, and now it was almost impossible to look away. There wasn't a single mile on this road that didn't hold a memory of her.

She caught him staring and shrank a little in self-consciousness. "Why are you staring?"

"You look different." It was only half the truth. She was so beautiful, and his heart ached for those years they spent together. Missing her was physically painful.

"Six years is a long time." She said it casually, but those six years felt like a lifetime.

"Did you change your look for a role you're working on?" He was curious about so much more than her change in looks, but he had to start somewhere.

"No," she hesitated. "I'm not acting anymore."

She said it without feeling. The emotion that the admission should have conjured was missing, and he was having trouble putting the pieces together. Acting was Lindsey's world, her passion. How could she not be acting?

"Um, what? Why?" he asked.

"I haven't been to an audition in three years." She didn't seem to care, and he felt like she should be at least a little upset. "Broadway just sort of... dimmed over time, and I found that I was interested in other things."

His little Lindsey had been consumed with the dream of becoming an actress. He couldn't imagine what could've caused this change.

"Did something happen..."

"No. No. Dakota, nothing bad happened." She rushed to explain then drew a deep breath before continuing. "I'm sorry... for what I did, how I left you.

I'm so sorry, Dakota. You were so good to me, and you were my best friend. I just…"

"You don't have to apologize to me, Lindz. You were doing what was best for you. I see that now, and I even saw it then. The fact that it hurt me was unfortunate, but inevitable."

"No, it wasn't inevitable. I shouldn't have left. I didn't see what I had here until it was gone, and then it was too late to get it back." Her voice broke on the last word.

"If you hadn't gone and at least tried to experience your dreams, you wouldn't have been happy here. You knew there was something else out there for you, and the longing wouldn't have stopped until you chased it down. I get it. I've had years to think about what happened, and I understand now. Trust me, it took a long time to understand, but now I do. I never blamed you for going after anything you wanted. I just wanted the chance to stand beside you through it all," he explained.

"I just couldn't ask you to come with me. You would have hated it. You belong here," she said.

"I would do anything for you, follow you anywhere, and be happy to do it," he confessed. He knew he wasn't speaking in past tense now, but he didn't care. She had a right to know how he felt.

"No, you wouldn't have been happy. What right did I have to take you away from the life you loved so I could do what I wanted to do?" Her voice rose as she asked.

"You had every right, and you know it. You never asked, but I offered just the same."

She scoffed. "That's because you would've done anything for me. Even if it meant living a life you would've hated."

"I would never hate a life where I got to spend every day with you."

She grew silent, and he let her be. He knew the bomb he'd just dropped on her was something she should've known anyway, but it hadn't been put into words before.

When they pulled into the parking lot at The Line and she put the car in park, Lindsey looked at him.

"I didn't spend those years chasing dreams like I thought I would. I spent them missing you and hating myself for ruining what we had. How could I enjoy anything without you there with me? No adventure was fun without you."

He knew what she meant. Anything they did together was easy and exciting. Having to go through life without her had been torture.

"I wanted you to be happy. I wanted you to have everything you ever wanted, Lindz. You had those big city eyes, and I couldn't compete with that."

"I know. You wanted me to be happy enough that you let me go. Can you understand that I let you go for the same reason?" She turned her body to face him in the tiny car seat, and they were close enough to feel the warmth of each other's breath.

He did understand, but it was all coming together

too late. The realization was dawning for both of them. She was his home, and he should have made that clear six years ago. Her lips were so close now, and he couldn't focus on anything else.

He closed the gap between them, rested his forehead against hers, and cupped her face. He let her scent fill him as he gave in to the euphoria of her presence. She even smelled the same, and his heart leapt at the recognition of sugar and sunshine. She'd always smelled like sweet summertime.

He swallowed hard past the lump in his throat. "I missed you, Lindz. We lost so much."

"I know. That was my fault. Let's just enjoy now while we can," she pleaded.

As they exited the car, he felt the uneasy weight of her words.

While we can.

She would leave again, and as much as he knew it would rip him apart, he couldn't help following her into the restaurant wishing they weren't living on borrowed time.

CHAPTER 11
Lindsey

She was transported back in time as she entered the cafeteria-style restaurant and stopped short, causing Dakota to bump into her. His hands grabbed her waist to steady her, and now she was paralyzed for a new and exciting reason. His touch felt like fire, and she gave an involuntary shiver then resisted the urge to melt into him.

"Whoa, what's the hold up?" He was so close to her, she could feel the heat from his breath in her ear.

It took a moment for her thoughts to compose.

Shake it off, Lindz. Don't get distracted by him. Everything here is temporary. "Um. It's just that this place hasn't changed... at all."

His laugh was a welcome sound, and oh how she missed it. "Well, if it ain't broke, don't fix it, right?"

He stepped around her but grabbed her hand as he passed, pulling her toward the line of customers waiting to be served.

Her heart leapt at the touch, and she sucked in a deep breath as she allowed herself to follow behind him.

Holding hands was an intimate gesture to her, and Dakota knew that. When she confessed it to him years ago, he told her he understood. He said he thought of it as a way to link himself to her when they were in public. Interlocking their fingers reminded him that they were fused together, connected for the world to see. It was his small way to *feel* the support they carried for each other, and she'd found it endearing. The crazy part was that he explained the feeling she hadn't been able to put into words herself. His revelation made the elementary action feel significant. She'd only known that holding hands with him had felt wonderful and right, but he understood, and maybe that was the reason why it only felt that way with him.

She really had stepped back in time. The problem was that you couldn't go back and recapture the past once it was lost. The ticking of the clock changes everything. The things she was experiencing now were the same, but she was seeing through jaded eyes with longer shadows and recalled memories. The present lacked the ache for the future because it had arrived. She and Dakota were living the lives they'd once pushed forward to inherit. The ache for what had once belonged to her seared her heart.

He stopped behind the elderly couple waiting at the back of the line and pointed to the chalkboard where the day's menu was written. "What'll it be, Lindz?"

Her emotions were playing a cruel joke on her today, and it was exhausting. She'd loved the stability of her relationship with Dakota all those years ago, and the highs and lows she experienced with him now just felt wrong.

They had something special and innocent back then, and she ruined it by allowing the world to enter their bubble of happiness. She lost herself out there, and in turn lost a relationship that meant the world to her.

He squeezed her hand and the grin that had fallen from her face returned as she studied the menu.

"You're kidding. They still have chicken and dumplings on Thursdays? Does nothing change around here?" she asked playfully. Why was the past always so close here?

"I'm pretty sure the working folk in town who live for Thursday dumplings would riot if they heard you complaining." He crossed his arms over his broad chest and leaned back to grin at her.

"I'm not complaining. You know it's my favorite." Why was she reminding him of her preferences? *He doesn't care anymore.*

"That's why things don't change around here," he said.

Everything was the same, except Dakota. She couldn't forget his revelation about the person he'd been all those years ago.

He's gone.

He was right. Some things shouldn't change, and she could feel it between them now. They were the same people they'd always been. Sure, they'd grown, learned, and experienced, but they *were* essentially the same.

She wanted to take his words and reject them, call them out as false. The chasm of time between them dissipated, and the natural way they fell into place beside each other took its place.

Lindsey had been unsure back then. She'd been young and full of energy and longing for *more*. She didn't know what she wanted, but she knew she wanted to try something different.

She couldn't remember a time in her life when New York hadn't been her dream. She wanted to go places, see new things, meet new people. She wanted to see the world, and all she'd ever known was Carson. The lights, the noise, the music. New York called to her.

Now, she could see that obsession for what it was—her downfall. The things that drew her to the big city were the same things that pulled her away from God. She was ashamed to admit how easily she'd been pulled away from her Heavenly Father, how easily she turned her back on an eternity of happiness for the flash of the New York lights.

She knew the city wasn't to blame. It had only been a distraction. A distraction she should've been able to overcome. If she'd only kept her heart with

God, she could've lived in the city and been happy. But her love of the world was strong, and it overpowered her relationship with God.

When she graduated from high school, she took classes at the community college in town during the summer. Her intention was to take her associate degree in liberal arts to a university and get a bachelor's degree, but that idea seemed bland and took a backseat to the dream of becoming an actor sometime during that first term. The image of stardom and being a part of something bigger overshadowed anything college had to offer her, and she decided to move to New York City when she was barely nineteen years old.

Dakota had been twenty and spent every spare minute working since he was sixteen. He was smart, but college hadn't appealed to him. They lived in a rural, working town, and there were plenty of manual labor jobs to snatch up for a young, strong boy willing to work hard for a decent wage.

Dakota was happy with his life here, and although he couldn't understand her need to move to New York, he never tried to stop her. Support was his middle name, and he never faltered. A man like Dakota was rare, and the realization stuck in her gut like a hot knife.

They passed through the line and ordered their food without speaking to each other. When they reached the cashier, Dakota quickly paid for her meal before she could protest.

"Thank you for that. You didn't have to buy my meal," she said.

"Of course I did. You're my date."

He was so sure he didn't even bat an eye.

"Um..."

"I'm kidding. I know this isn't a date, but let a man dream." He gave her a wink accompanied by a flirtatious grin. She was powerless against his charms as she felt her cheeks heat. It was suddenly sweltering in the tiny restaurant.

She sat beside Dakota, half paralyzed with some irrational fear of how strong her feelings still were for him. She felt feverish, chilled, her heart was beating out of her chest, and her joints seemed to have stepped out to lunch. She was falling apart in front of him, and he was as cool as a cucumber.

They ate in silence for a little while, both people watching like they used to do whenever they ate at The Line. The sweet tea was divine, and she made sure to tell him how much she missed the sugary drink during her time up north. Of all the allures of New York, it lacked southern charm.

She scanned the restaurant and spotted her old nemesis just as Dakota raised his eyebrows and tilted his head casually to his right. Ms. Miller was making her way toward their table. She was a snake of a woman who had always believed Dakota hung the moon and Lindsey was some vile creature meant to steal joy.

"Oh, no. Dakota, do something," Lindsey whispered and tried to keep her face turned from Ms.

Miller's prying eyes. She knew the plea was useless, but she was desperate and not even close to being in a good enough mindset to trade insults with the nasty Ms. Miller.

"Little Lindsey, is that you? My goodness, you look downright homely with that hairstyle. Hasn't anyone told you?"

Her words were like fire in Lindsey's veins. Her breathing came in shorter, quicker bursts, and she was powerless to stop it. How could she possibly think that was an appropriate greeting?

Ms. Miller's own auburn curls were clearly dyed and cared for by a professional stylist on a regular basis. The hairspray-drenched curls stood four inches tall and four inches from her temples, never touching her face in any way. They were suspended in air and were a testament to the power of professional hair products.

Lindsey couldn't afford hair products these days, nor could she afford to dye her hair or visit a salon often. Her hair hung loosely in her natural color, and that was all she had to offer. She liked her hair this way, but the people of this town remembered her with short, straight, blonde hair, and that was the way it should be in their eyes. Anything else was rejected.

When she was younger, she would have snapped back at Ms. Miller without a second thought, but her maturity kept her silent now. That and the unshed tears pricking the back of her eyes that she refused to let see the light of day.

"I think her hair is beautiful. It just goes to show

that some women just have it and some have to pay for it," Dakota said. His tone wasn't rude, but his words were meant to sting the pretentious Ms. Miller.

Ms. Miller looked at him and visibly jumped back as if she'd been slapped. "Why, I never. Dakota, you know I admire you, but you have strange taste." She pursed her lips, causing the wrinkles around her mouth to deepen, and looked back to Lindsey. "What are you doing back here anyway, child?"

She barely found her voice. "My friend, Sissy, had a baby girl this week. I came to help take care of the baby until things settle down."

Ms. Miller's wrinkled mouth twisted to the left. "Well, I'm sure Sissy is fully capable of caring for her own children."

Dakota inserted himself into the conversation again. "She definitely is, but Lindsey is such a pleasure to have around, we were thinking of asking her to move back for good, right, Lindz?" Dakota was stirring the pot so easily now as he gave her a wink with his steel-blue eyes that requested she play along.

"I've been thinking of setting up shop here. I think this town needs a little bit of nightly entertainment." She could play this game. This was much easier than biting her tongue.

"What're you talkin' 'bout? Nightly entertainment?" Ms. Miller's southern drawl came out in full force when she was riled up. Lindsey and Dakota had laughed many times at the crazy words she could come up with that you would never find in a dictionary.

"Didn't you hear? Lindsey is a burlesque dancer in Vegas now. She's the star of her own show." Dakota nodded at her excitedly, and she was having trouble reining in the giggles.

"What's a burlesque dancer? Is that like those showgirls with the feathers and bikinis, or is that a fancy word for stripper?" Ms. Miller asked in an astonished whisper, her eyes growing wide.

"Sort of, but we wear fewer feathers and less..." Lindsey paused for dramatic effect. "Just less than a show girl and more than a stripper. You know what I mean? I've been on the big stage for years now." She acted proud, and Ms. Miller's face began to turn pink.

"You're trying to tell me you want to bring your filthy dance show to Carson?" The volume of her voice was drawing attention now, and Lindsey decided it was time to rein in the joke.

"Nah, it was just a passing thought. Don't get me wrong, I would love to come home. I just don't want to leave my big fancy Vegas show." She sold the lie like a champ and looked to Dakota for approval.

His mouth was hanging open slightly, and he was staring at her like she was a unicorn. Maybe she'd taken the fib too far. His hand holding his glass of sweet tea hung suspended in the air. "Uh, yeah. She's got a pretty good gig, and... um, what?" Dakota fumbled over his words, and she finally let the giggle escape. The whole charade had been fun, but now it was time to let it go.

"See you later, Ms. Miller." Lindsey waved and

dismissed the busybody.

Dakota was still staring at her after Ms. Miller stormed out of the restaurant. His blue eyes contrasted beautifully with his tan skin and dark hair. They were tiny pools of light in the darkness.

"Thanks for that." She nodded her head toward the door where Ms. Miller had made her escape.

"No problem," he said, but he was still staring at her.

"What?" she asked.

A smile crept over his face. "I can't believe we did that. I'm going to have to call the preacher and let him know it isn't true. She's probably calling him as we speak."

Her mouth dropped open. "Oh no. I forgot she has the preacher on speed dial."

"You'll be on the prayer list this week."

"Stop it." She threw her napkin at his head, and he let it hit the floor without reaching.

His deep laugh was music to her ears. "I really do like your new hairstyle. It reminds me of when you were young."

"Thanks. I know it's quite a change, but I'm used to it. I went back to my natural color years ago," she shared as she resumed eating her own meal.

"I'm glad you like it too. I want you to be happy. Even if it means being a burlesque dancer in Vegas." His grin twitched right before he shoved another spoonful of food in his mouth.

She rolled her eyes. "I said stop it. You know I've

always been fairly modest." Her unwillingness to take on the more risqué roles had been one of the factors that drove her out of show business so quickly.

"You're right. You would never make it as a showgirl." He shook his head in mock disappointment.

"I could too... if I wanted to. It just so happens I have no desire to be a showgirl," her voice was rising in her need to prove him wrong as usual. "But I could totally be a showgirl if I wanted to."

Dakota chuckled and looked around. "Okay, I get it." He put his hands up in surrender and laughed. "You're killing me."

"If I wanted to kill you, I would have hit you with my car the day I got back into town. I had a perfect opportunity," she jested.

"I figured you were still mad, but I'm glad you decided to spare my life. I guess I'm in your debt."

"Look, Dakota. I'm sorry about that. I wasn't paying attention, and then I should have handled the situation better. I was... caught off guard. I wasn't ready to face you and what I'd done." She stared at her food because she couldn't bear to look at him right now. Her guilt had been weighing on her, and she needed to get things off her chest.

"All is forgiven. I think it's been proven that I can't stay mad at you."

He was forgiving her so easily and making her feel things that would send her spiraling when the time came to leave this place. Her heart hurt to even think about leaving.

His words interrupted her gloomy thoughts, "So, if you're not acting now, and I'm assuming you're not a burlesque dancer in Vegas, what are you up to?"

She could hear the blatant intrigue in his voice, and a part of her couldn't wait to tell him.

She smiled in anticipation of his reaction. "I'm a bookkeeper at a law firm in Raleigh."

He certainly hadn't expected that answer. "You're a what?"

"A bookkeeper handles the financial dealings of—"

"I know what a bookkeeper is, Lindz. What I don't understand is how you're a bookkeeper."

"Well, I went back to college and got a degree in accounting. Oh, and I do some tax work during season for extra income," she added.

"I didn't... is that what you wanted to do?" he asked, almost confused.

"It wasn't at first. I *did* want to perform, but jobs were hard to come by, and I was falling into debt. I just knew I couldn't continue to let myself sink deeper into that hole, and really, I wasn't happy. It was stressful during the times when I didn't have a gig. I didn't want to live my life never knowing where my next paycheck was coming from, you know?" She tapped her fork on her plate and whispered, "And I knew I wasn't supposed to be there. I was... lost."

"I... I can see where that was hard." He paused to run his hand through his short hair. "I'm sorry, Lindz. If you needed help, you could have just called me."

"No, I couldn't call you. One of the reasons I

wanted to go in the first place was because I didn't want to be dependent on you my entire life. I wanted to show everyone, mostly myself, that I could do something on my own. I can't remember a time in my life where we didn't do everything together. Dakota and Lindsey did this, or Dakota and Lindsey did that. *Lindsey* never did anything herself."

She realized her voice was raised and sat back in her chair to calm the wake inside of her. He sat staring at her for a moment, and she could see the indecision in him. He almost seemed... hurt.

"I never wanted you to feel like you were tied to me like that. You could've just told me you wanted some space, or some independence."

"I know. I know now it would've been that simple." Why did that realization hurt so much?

"For what it's worth, I'm proud of you." She looked up to find him looking at her like she held the answer to the question of life, the universe, and everything. "You were always so good at math and problem solving, and this makes all the sense in the world. It suits you just right."

"I would like to think I benefited from doing your math homework all through eighth grade," she added.

"I'm so glad I could help."

His acceptance meant more than it should, and she felt lighter without the secrecy of the turn her life plan had taken. She would never know why she felt the crushing need to share things with him that mattered to her.

CHAPTER 12
Dakota

They finished their meals, and Dakota took her hand in his as they exited the restaurant like it was the most natural thing to do. Something instinctual made him reach for her, begged to touch her in even the smallest of ways. He needed to be connected to her, even if it was only their hands touching.

"You need new tires, Lindz," he pointed out as he opened the driver's side door for her to enter.

"Yeah, I keep forgetting to do that. I'll take care of it."

"We can drop it off at Marcus' shop tomorrow. He'll fix you up quick. I'll make sure he has the tires." He pulled his phone from his pocket and texted Marcus.

"I'm not really in a position this month to splurge on tires. I'm still digging out of debt." Her confession was almost inaudible, and he knew it hurt her to admit it.

"Tires are not a frivolous expense. You *need* new tires, and you're getting them tomorrow." He didn't look up from his phone.

"I told you, I—"

"I heard you, but I also just told Marcus to put it on my account. Problem solved."

"Dakota! Didn't you just hear my spiel about needing independence from you?" she asked incredulously.

"I did, and consider this a thank you for helping Sissy out this week. She needs her friend right now, and I think we'll all rest easier knowing you're here to support her."

"I didn't come here for any gifts or payment," she added.

"I know you didn't. You came because you love your friend, and you're just that selfless. I get it. But I need you to know how much it has meant to all of us that you're here, especially since I messed up and went AWOL for a few days." She hadn't signed up to pull him back on the wagon. He owed her for keeping Sissy from losing her cool.

In all honesty, he just wanted to do something for her. He wanted to show her how much she meant to him. He wanted to help her in any little way he could. Sure, he knew she didn't need him. She'd done a good job with her life without him for years. She went back to college and made a career doing something she loved, and he admired her for it.

"I'll find some way to repay you," she conceded. "I'll help with your taxes next year or something."

"Deal." Any excuse to see her again felt like hope.

They pulled up at Sissy's a few minutes later and entered quietly in case Sissy and Lydia were still napping.

He stepped in behind Lindsey and heard Sissy giggling in the living area. He was immensely thankful to hear that sound. "What's so funny, Sis?" he asked.

Sissy was sitting in the recliner with her feet crossed under her, holding Lydia slightly above her lap so they were face to face. Tears were rolling down Sissy's face, and she was having trouble catching her breath. Thankfully, they were happy tears. "She's out like a light and making the funniest spit bubbles I've ever seen." She fell into another round of breathless laughter, squeezing her eyes closed tight.

The sight of Sissy laughing like a hyena came over him suddenly, and he tried to suppress the laugh he felt building in his chest. Surely, it was just relief he felt for Sissy, but the sight was hilarious.

Lindsey didn't hinder her laughter and gave in to the giggles. Soon they were laughing at each other, and he was thankful for this moment.

Lindsey was beautiful on a bad day. She was gorgeous when she laughed without a care in the world. If he could stop time, this would be the moment to keep.

Sissy adjusted her hands to hold Lydia on one side so she could wipe her tears. "Oh, I needed that. I feel a little more like myself now." She sniffed and attempted to pull herself back together.

Lindsey brushed her friend's stray hairs behind her ear and said, "I know it's been tough lately, but the doctor said it takes time for things to even back out after you have a baby."

Lindsey had always been an optimist of the highest order. She just knew things were going to work out, and she did everything in her power to make sure it happened. There was something to be said about her go-getter attitude. Everything she was, everything she did, made her into the wonderful woman he adored.

Why did the woman of his dreams have to be her —the unattainable one? The woman who didn't want him was the only woman he wanted. He couldn't even see other women.

And then she did something that stopped him cold. Lindsey reached for the sleeping Lydia and held her bundled body close.

Alarms were sounding in his head. He'd resorted to the numbing alcohol the last time he saw Lindsey holding Lydia at the hospital, but this time felt different and scarier.

He wanted to be with Lindsey, and he wanted a family. But God's will so far hadn't afforded him either. He'd always known that she was the one for him, and he'd wondered for years why God saw something different for him. It had taken years to accept that God didn't *want* him to be unhappy. Things just didn't always work out the way we want them to.

Even before she left, he knew he wanted to spend the rest of his life with her, grow old with her, go through life with her. He'd wanted many things with her in life, but he hadn't thought about a baby before.

Lindsey just looked right with a sleeping infant in her arms. They hadn't really talked about kids before, and a new fear stacked on top of the old ones. Not only would he lose her again, but the perfect woman would walk out of his life, and she would take any hope of a family with her. God knew his heart and could see that he had no desire for marriage or a family with anyone else.

He'd never been controlling, possessive, or jealous before, but in this moment, he felt a little of all three of those things. What if she'd fallen in love with someone else in the years she'd been gone? What if she left this week and then found someone else?

The thought of Lindsey with someone else hurt him more than it should. He knew the thought wasn't rational or called for, but he couldn't control the way he felt.

Never before had he felt the need to connect with someone so fiercely.

He needed a chance to think, and he knew he couldn't think rationally here watching Lindsey holding Lydia. He felt... unprepared. He felt like he needed a plan, but he wasn't sure what the plan even meant to accomplish yet.

"Um, well, Lydia looks like a little angel, so I guess I'd better go. I have some errands to run." It was a lie. He needed some time to himself.

"I'll drive you home," Lindsey offered.

"No." His response came out too fast and sounded offensive. "I'll get Tyler to drop me off." He wasn't ready to bring Lindsey home yet.

He saw the worry Sissy tried to hide as she said, "Why don't you get him out of this house? I know he's probably itching for a minute to do something other than change diapers and tend to Lydia and me."

"You sure?" he asked.

"Totally. We need some girl time anyway, don't we, Lindz?" Sissy gave an obvious wink, making it clear that she wanted all the details of their lunch date that was not a real date. Forget it, he was definitely going to think of it as a date, whether Lindsey liked it or not.

The baby gave a small whimper as she woke, and Lindsey handed her back to Sissy.

"She needs to eat. I'm going to have to ask you to leave." Leave it to Sissy to know how to run him off.

He held up his hands in surrender. "I'm out. Bye."

Sissy called out, "Ty is in the garage out back," as he left the room.

He found Tyler sitting in his bass boat with lures and worms spread out on the deck around him.

"Hey, man, everything okay with Lindz?" Tyler

asked pleasantly as if he hadn't kicked him out of the house in a fury a few hours ago.

"Oh yeah, man. We're fine. Just hadn't had a chance to talk things out yet."

"Good. Sissy has been worried about this reunion for months. Now, I know why." Tyler stashed his fishing rods in the locker of the boat and turned back to face him. "What is it about Lindsey that kept you hanging on for so many years?"

That was a loaded question. "Where do I start? She's fun, drop-dead gorgeous, insanely smart, selfless, and deeply passionate about anything she loves, including God. She's the total package, and the only woman I've ever loved or will ever love. She's the one, and she always will be."

He didn't know how God wove their fates into being, but he was certain no one got to choose who they loved in this life. There were a million reasons to love Lindsey, and he was powerless to resist any of them. No one else ever held a candle to her, for whatever reason. It had always been her.

"Well, don't hold back," Tyler joked.

"I mean it. I thought I'd idealized her all these years she's been gone. I thought maybe I'd built her up to be something greater than she really was. Now I know I was stupid to think that. Of course, she's as sweet and nice as I remembered. I was hung up on her for a reason, and after spending the day with her, I know she's really the only woman I'll ever love." Dakota leaned over the railing of the boat and crossed his arms to watch Tyler pack up his baits.

"What are you gonna do?" Ty asked with all the understanding of Dakota's dilemma.

"I don't know. I need some time to think about it. When I told Sissy I was heading out, she asked me to bring you along. She said you need a break, but really she wanted you to keep an eye on me."

"Do you need a guardian?" Ty asked half joking. Sure, it sounded silly that Sissy would worry about him like that, but he was the one who had given her a reason.

"No, actually, I'm fine. Since you've got some free time, want to throw some lines at the lake?" He and Tyler fished together as often as they could. They both had busy schedules, but they snuck away whenever the chance presented itself. They usually found time to night fish about once a week.

"Yes. I don't think I'll be getting to fish much more now that Lydia's here. I'd better take advantage of Lindsey being here to help." Tyler jumped off the boat, and they grabbed their gear.

If he needed a chance to think about how to handle his feelings for Lindsey, a fishing trip was the best way to do it.

He and Tyler fished well together because their styles matched, but more importantly, they both had very little to say on the water. Fishing was a sport of leisure and relaxation for them, and that's exactly what he needed.

CHAPTER 13
Lindsey

"Spill your guts. I'm sick of watching soap operas and reality TV. If I have to hear about another secret baby, I'm going to lose my mind." Sissy barely waited until Dakota closed the back door to question Lindsey.

"We actually had a great time. We went to The Line, and we ran into Ms. Miller."

Sissy gasped in horror. "Tell me more. Did she slip and fall in front of everyone? She would deserve it." Sissy had always sided with Lindsey in the never-ending face-off between Little Lindsey and the infamous Ms. Miller.

"Sissy! That's not nice." Not nice was an understatement, but she knew Sissy's heart wasn't mean. She just tended to look out for her friend's feelings. "But we did feed her a satisfying story that probably had her running to tattle to the preacher."

"Go on." Sissy's mischievous smile grew. Her

friend was a genuinely good person, and it just made sense to her that kindness was easier and no one should waste the energy to be nasty to someone else. In Sissy's eyes, if Ms. Miller was going to stick to her awful attitude, she deserved to pay for it.

"I told her I was a burlesque dancer, and I was thinking of opening a show here in town."

"Oh, that's funny. You know she's going to have the entire congregation praying for your lost soul." She hugged the nursing Lydia to her chest a little tighter and laughed again. "Oh, she's definitely telling everyone in town as we speak. Your reputation is ruined. You'll never find a suitable husband now," Sissy quipped.

"Then it's a good thing it's not the eighteenth century and I'm not thinking about marriage," Lindsey said. If she was being honest, she had been thinking... about Dakota.

She knew pining after him would be like pouring gasoline on the fire, but it was impossible to push him from her mind. He was just as thoughtful, caring, charming, funny, and understanding as he'd always been. Now, he was even more selfless and kind. She was in trouble.

"Are you really not looking?" Sissy asked worriedly. It wasn't that Sissy believed a woman could only be happy attached to a man. She knew her friend secretly wished she and Dakota would somehow live happily ever after.

"Well, I wasn't. I haven't dated anyone to speak of

in years. I really haven't had a relationship with anyone that had lasting power since Dakota," she admitted.

"Exactly. Does he still have a chance?"

"Are we going to talk about this? Really?" It was inevitable. Sissy seemed to know everything. Tyler must have spilled the beans about the kiss.

"Um, no and yes. Keep it G-rated because he's my brother, but are y'all falling in love again?" Sissy had no filter.

Lindsey sighed. "We kissed yesterday, but he was drunk, and it was definitely a mistake. He regretted it. I could tell." It still hurt to talk about that rejection, but who else could she confide in if not her friend?

"I seriously doubt that, but the question is do *you* regret it?"

"Not until I realized what it meant to him. He was angry... with me. Afterward, it almost seemed like a punishment. I mean it seemed like he wanted to remind me of what we had, what we were together, just so he could hurt me by taking it away," Lindsey explained.

"I can tell you, in all honesty, that Dakota did not do that. I know what he feels for you, and he doesn't want to punish you for anything you did for yourself or to him. Has he ever treated you like that before?" Sissy asked as she gazed at her daughter adoringly.

"No, never," she confessed.

"I'm guessing it hasn't occurred to you that he may have been disappointed in himself for the way he handled the situation? Or could he have been the one hurting? I mean, maybe he kissed you then realized you are just going to leave him again."

"Oh no," Lindsey covered her face with her hands and hung her head between her knees.

She really hadn't thought about how it must have been for him. She raised her head and wondered aloud, "How could I have been so self-centered?"

"You're not self-centered. You're dealing with your own set of uncertainties. It's hard to look at things from all sides when you're stuck in the middle. I'm not saying he's without fault. I'm saying maybe there is more to the reaction than what you perceived."

"How will I ever know what he feels without just outright asking him? We're getting more comfortable with sharing, but we're not ready to just lay all our cards on the table yet. We're both a little jaded these days," Lindsey pointed out.

"I think you just need to get to know him again. Once you do, you'll really know how he feels. You won't have to ask."

Sissy had been a bystander for both sides of the breakup, and that meant she knew what they both needed in order to work things out. Her friend had stock in both sides, and it was in Sissy's best interest to help them through this.

A terrible thought popped into Lindsey's head for the first time. "What if he's seeing someone else?" Suddenly, her stomach rolled in protest. It would be her own fault if he had moved on.

"He kissed you yesterday. We can certainly rule out

a girlfriend." Of course, Sissy wasn't clouded by emotions, and she was obviously thinking more clearly.

Lindsey released the breath she'd been holding. "That's true. He has always been loyal."

"To a fault," Sissy added. "I can say with certainty that he hasn't loved anyone since you. I would know."

Well, that was certainly a heavy burden and a weight off her chest at the same time.

"He's taking my car to get tires tomorrow," Lindsey said.

"And that isn't a surprise at all. He's been dying for someone to care for, and you just happen to fit the bill perfectly." Sissy adjusted herself and moved Lydia to nurse on her other side.

"Why do I want to reject his gifts?" The question was rhetorical, and Sissy didn't answer. She was waiting for Lindsey to come to the realization herself.

"I have nothing to offer him."

Seeing that the baby was milk drunk again, Sissy positioned Lydia upright against her chest to coax a burp. "We know that's not true, but if you're not willing to open yourself up to him again, I can understand that. What the two of you had was all-consuming, and you've been living a solitary life for a long time now. Change is never easy, but trusting someone the way a relationship needs is scary."

Of course, Sissy was right, but the realization didn't make anything easier.

"I guess we should just take it day by day," Lindsey conceded.

"For three more days?" Sissy asked.

That was all she had. Three days left in this town, and then she would have to go back to the life she'd been living... alone.

Would they be three days of wishing and longing or three days of living in the moment and following her heart?

Lindsey woke the next morning more refreshed than she had been since arriving in Carson. She and Tyler were taking turns helping Sissy with night feedings, and last night was Tyler's turn.

Taking care of a newborn really did take a village. Lydia was a wonderful baby, but it was inevitable that she would wake numerous times throughout the night. She still slept most of the day and night, but she would wake about every five hours during the night to eat.

Since Sissy was adamant that she would try her best to breastfeed, she could pump small amounts throughout the day and have enough to be able to sleep through one of Lydia's wakings while Lindsey and Tyler took turns feeding Lydia from a bottle.

She didn't mind getting up in the night to spend half an hour with the sweet baby. Truthfully, a part of her looked forward to it, causing her to jump out of bed at the first whimper.

She knew this wasn't a real motherhood experience. Sissy was exhausted, and rightfully so. Her body was healing, her sleeping erratic, and she worried often.

Worry was a foreign concept to her friend. Sissy hadn't spent a single moment of her life in worry or doubt until Lydia came along. She knew Sissy wasn't voicing all of her internal troubles, but she often questioned whether Lydia was eating enough, if she should be sleeping so much, if she produced an ample amount of wet and dirty diapers, and other concerns that Lindsey could easily put to rest with the copious knowledge she'd acquired from the doctors and nurses recently.

Lindsey had the easy job of heating a refrigerated bottle of breastmilk and rocking Lydia in the quiet nursery until she returned to her favorite activity—sleeping.

Lindsey slept an uninterrupted ten hours last night, and her joints felt stiff. She would bet money that she hadn't moved at all throughout the night.

Her eyes adjusted to the muted sun diffusing through the translucent curtains, and she laid still and quiet to absorb the tranquility of the morning. The day was sure to be filled with excitement, whether it be surprises from the new baby, spending time with her best friend, or seeing Dakota again. He promised to come by before lunch so she could follow him to drop her car off at Marcus' shop.

Happiness filled her at the day's possibilities, and she threw the sheets and covers from her body, ready to jump into the action of the day. The prospect of spending time with Dakota sent her heart beating wildly, and she knew she couldn't spend these last days holding back her feelings.

She wanted to be open with Dakota. She wanted to live again, and she hadn't truly been herself since she left Carson. Being with him felt like waking up from a long, dreamless sleep.

Lindsey knew she would eventually have to consider the consequences of her carefree approach to their time together, but the thought of leaving just hurt. It nagged at her, but the need to feel the way Dakota made her feel was greater than the distant loss right now.

Haphazardly throwing the covers back on the bed in her haste to start the day, she worried that her decision to pursue a relationship with an expiration date with the man she never stopped loving would be a disaster.

She wondered if she could ever be the same after waking up again.

CHAPTER 14
Dakota

Lindsey's faded-red Maxima pulled into the gravel lot behind Dakota's Bronco at Brother's Automotive. He threw his truck into park, killed the engine, and stepped out before her vehicle came to a complete stop.

He was anxious, and it wasn't something he could easily hide. It was hot for October, but that didn't explain the sweat forming on his temples. She kept him on guard. That was the only explanation.

She stepped out of the car with the fluid motion of a dancer. Her wavy brown hair hung loose over her tan shoulders that were left exposed by her solid white tank top.

He loved the way she moved, and she seemed to have only perfected the action over time. Lindsey walked like she was suspended in water. She floated wherever she went, leaving him hypnotized in her wake.

She pushed her sunglasses into her hair and squinted against the sun. "So this is where Marcus works now? It seems fitting. He was always a mechanic," she remarked innocently, as if she hadn't just thumped him in the chest with her mere presence.

"He owns the place."

He reached for her hand out of instinct, and she took it without hesitation, stepping back to gauge the sincerity in his statement.

"Really? That's great." She scanned the area, taking in the building and lot.

Marcus worked hard to make the garage exactly what he wanted, and he knew his way around a vehicle before he knew how to tie his shoes. Even before Lindsey left, Marcus was a mechanic, and a good one at that. He could tell you anything you wanted to know about motorized vehicles, and he didn't stop there. He constantly found ways to teach himself new things.

"Yeah, he deserves it. He worked really hard, and now he's the best mechanic in Carson." He stopped with one hand on the office door and turned to her. "He's also the only one around who doesn't try to rip off the customers. It's sad, but it's true."

She smiled. "Sounds like Marcus."

She would understand why Marcus insisted on practicing fair business. He hadn't been dealt the best hand in life, and he'd worked his way up from rock bottom to where he was today. Marcus didn't take shortcuts, and he didn't depend on anyone else. He treated people right and felt he deserved the same in return. In fact, it occurred to him that Marcus was a pretty solid model of the Golden Rule: Do unto others as you would have them do unto you.

He shoved the door open and led her into the office. Marcus sat behind the desk tapping on a dirty calculator.

"Hey, man." Dakota reached a hand out as Marcus stood to grasp it.

"Got your tires stacked on the floor by the vending machine. Take a look and make sure you like 'em."

Dakota half turned to Lindsey and said, "Be right back," before stepping out the door on the other side of Marcus' desk that led to the shop floor. The sounds of metal tinging against metal and the slamming of a car hood greeted him as he entered the garage. The smell of oil and metal was overpowering, but Marcus' employees never seemed to complain. Marcus was a fair boss, and his employees preferred to stick around.

He found the stack of tires beside the vending machine, and of course, they were top of the line. He requested the best for Lindsey's car, and he trusted Marcus to set her up right. He didn't care that they were a little on the expensive side.

He stepped back into the office just as Marcus asked Lindsey, "So, how long you staying?"

She looked uncomfortable for a second and averted her eyes. "I'll head back home Sunday evening."

"Where is home these days?" Marcus asked as he

leaned back in his office chair and locked his fingers behind his head in a relaxed position.

"Holly Springs, North Carolina. I work in Raleigh, but I live about thirty minutes outside the city."

Dakota silently wondered why she would live in a suburb instead of the metropolitan area, especially if she worked in the city. When did she leave New York?

"What brought you to North Carolina?" Marcus didn't have a problem using the twenty questions technique to get answers, and Dakota was grateful. He was learning things about her with every question Marcus asked.

Marcus was a man of few words. If he was talking, he was either leading you to what he wanted or tricking you into revealing something you normally wanted to hide.

"My mother moved there after she divorced Dad." She picked at her fingernails that she kept trimmed short. "I just thought maybe she needed me. I didn't want her to be alone." She huffed and laughed in the same breath. "She showed me how much she needed me when she met a man six months later and moved to California with him." She rolled her eyes. "Kids these days."

"You like it there?"

She lifted and settled one shoulder. "It's fine. I like my job. I like my apartment..." She paused to consider the question. "It's fine," she repeated.

"Just fine? What kind'a job you got?" Marcus sat

forward, propping his elbows on the desk and tenting his fingers as he listened intently.

"I'm a bookkeeper for a law firm. It's pretty steady."

He noticed she sounded like it was just any old job. She sounded content, but not overly attached.

Dakota leaned back against the wall, crossed his arms, and made a mental note to take lessons from Marcus on the art of gaining information.

The door to the shop opened and Cody Henderson stepped one foot into the office. Dakota's shoulders tensed and he lifted his chin.

Dakota. Despised. Cody Henderson.

He could feel his breathing coming harder as his chest tightened. Cody had never taken any pains to hide his crush on Lindsey. When he was younger and hot headed, Dakota had come to blows over Lindsey a few times. It just so happened that every one of those fights were with Cody.

Dakota was a man now and knew violence was useless and wrong, but Cody's cocky demeanor crawled under his skin. It didn't help that the guy couldn't take a hint.

Dakota had always been able to keep him at a reasonable distance, but it wasn't because he sat on his hands while Cody was around. Cody was the exact same height as Dakota and almost as broad. He had a slender nose, light-brown eyes, and an immature attitude even now. Dakota often wished the guy's presence didn't threaten him, but his wish had yet to be granted. He wouldn't give Cody a second glance, if he would just move on and leave Lindsey alone.

"Hey, boss, what's the word on the Maxima out front?" Cody asked Marcus before he even noticed Dakota and Lindsey.

Marcus pointed his No. 2 pencil at Lindsey. "Little Lindsey needs new tires. They're stacked by the vending machine." His pencil rotated in the direction of the tires.

"Lindsey Payne? No way, I can't believe it's you." Cody's face lit up like a Christmas tree as he stepped into the tiny office and made his way toward Lindsey.

Dakota felt the urge to wipe the smirk off Cody's face before remembering that violence always did more harm than good. He needed to take a deep breath and remember his morals. He'd come a long way from the boy who used to settle his battles with fists.

When Cody wrapped Lindsey in a more-than-friendly bear hug, Dakota's vision narrowed until all he could see was red. He pushed off the wall and cracked his knuckles in anticipation. There wasn't a chance in the world Cody hadn't seen him as he walked by. The guy was just that bold.

"Henderson, long time." Dakota stepped closer to them and his voice was low and stern.

Cody released Lindsey and gave Dakota a quick, "Hey," before turning back to Lindsey.

"Ride with me to pull your car around," Cody said, not taking his eyes off her as he stepped around her toward the parking lot.

Lindsey, oblivious to Cody's intentions, ran her hand down Dakota's arm from his elbow to his hand, leaving chills in its wake.

"I'll be right back, and we can get lunch." When she smiled at him like he was the only one she saw, he relaxed the smallest fraction.

"Anything you want." He meant every word. He would go to the ends of the earth for her. Dakota let her go, but not before giving Cody a warning glare.

He turned around to find Marcus shaking his head. "Some people just don't learn their lesson."

Dakota actually smiled. "Fair warning, I'm gonna have to set him straight."

"Just make sure he can physically show up for work. I need all hands on deck."

"Got it. I'm not in the game of rearranging faces anymore. I hope I don't have to ask for forgiveness for that again." Dakota moved to stand in the doorway and propped his hands on the doorframe above his head as he watched Cody put the moves on Lindsey while they moved her car. "How do you stand to work with that guy?"

"I don't. He finally figured out that I don't talk back and leaves me alone now. He just likes to get under your skin... and he likes Lindsey. I imagine it's a win-win for him," Marcus pointed out. "It's not like you two are together anyway. What's the big deal?"

Marcus knew all about the big deal. He was just trying to draw Dakota's attention to his ridiculous possessive display.

"She's always been my girl. I'm not letting her go this time." Dakota's mind was made up. He would fight for her... again. This time he would win.

Marcus didn't argue. "She doesn't seem too attached to her life in North Carolina, but does she know what you're doing?"

"Not yet, but she will soon." Dakota had a plan. It was hasty and rash, but their clock was ticking. He couldn't afford to wait much longer. She would be leaving in just a few days, if he didn't do something soon.

"Oh, really?" Marcus was eager to know Dakota's plan. Marcus was a thinker, a planner of the highest order. He never went in half-cocked.

When Dakota watched her Maxima pull into an open shop bay, he turned back to give Marcus his attention. "I'm going to convince her that there are more reasons to stay than to go back."

"How you plan on doing that, brother?"

The big plan wasn't so elaborate, but it would make the statement he intended.

"I'm taking her home."

He looked to the passenger seat to find her smiling. He didn't always know what caused those random, beautiful smiles, but he was grateful for every one he was allowed to experience. Her smile was one of his many weaknesses she controlled. He still remembered how those lips felt against his.

"What's got you so happy?" he asked.

"You still drive the Bronco," her smile didn't waver, but his fell instantly.

He turned his attention back to the road. "Not exactly."

"What do you mean?"

He wasn't ready for this conversation. Start with the good, then break the bad. "This is Bronco 2.0. The old one just didn't hold up."

It wasn't a lie, but he was stalling for time. He didn't want to tell her, but he knew it was coming. Someone else would tell her first, if he didn't do it soon.

"You didn't want something new? Really, that Bronco had seen its better days *before* I left." At least she was making it into a joke. She wasn't wrong, and his old vehicle was just that. Old.

"Nah. I liked the Bronco, so I decided to stick with it."

"Same two-tone green and white and everything? You really don't handle change well."

"For your information, I have another truck too, but is it really so bad that I know what I want?" he asked.

She considered his question. He felt the same way about most things in life. If he found something he liked, loved, or just worked for him, he stuck with it. Since when was loyalty and decisiveness a bad thing?

She reached for his hand, surprising him. Her fingers were delicate and soft against his calloused palms.

"It's not a bad thing at all. I like that you know what you want. I wish I was as grounded as you. Sometimes, I don't know what I really want, or worse, I don't have the courage to actually stand up and pursue what I want."

He huffed. "That's new. You've always been a go-getter. What changed?"

"I was the little fish in a huge ocean for years. Being on the bottom doesn't exactly inspire someone like me to just get up and take what she wants."

He hated hearing her doubt herself. Her fire had seemed inextinguishable. "You're capable of anything, Lindz. I've seen you fearless, remember? You can have that again. I remember a time when nothing would have kept you from going after what you wanted."

"I know. Life just kicks you while you're down sometimes, and it's hard to stand back up and fight again."

Silence filled the cab of the truck until they stopped at the brick building housing the pizza bar they had agreed on for lunch. They both had a lot to think about, but the silence felt full instead of empty.

He killed the engine as she turned to him.

"Kota. I'm gonna get it back. My drive. It's just that things are confusing right now, and I'm... scared." Her gaze dropped to her lap as she fiddled with her fingers.

He pulled her chin up to catch her attention. Her striking eyes always surprised him. They were drops of chocolate and a direct opposite to his steel-blue.

"I get it, Lindz. Just promise me you'll keep your options open until you know for sure what you really want." He stroked his thumb over her smooth cheek and wished he could stop time. He prayed she'd choose him. Prayed choosing him would be the best thing for both of them and what God had planned.

"I will." She smiled, and he reluctantly let her go.

CHAPTER 15
Lindsey

The food at Jerry's Pizza Bar was amazing. She couldn't remember the last time she tasted something so delicious. Despite the name, the Pizza Bar was known for its shredded ham hoagies. Her entire mouth tingled with happiness as she closed her eyes and moaned her appreciation. Grease seeped from the saturated bun onto her fingers.

"Mmm. I missed this so much," she said through a mouth full of ham and mayonnaise.

Dakota gave a deep chuckle. "I knew you'd love it."

His gaze never left hers, intimidating her, as he took another bite and chewed slowly. She knew he was trying to get under her skin. There was a time when they could look into each other's eyes and almost perceive the other's thoughts. Right now, she was sure he'd used the word *love* to force her to think about the feeling.

He leaned forward as if pulled to her by an invisible string, and she took the opportunity to gently place her hand on top of his. She needed to change the subject before she actually ended up thinking about the emotion... again.

She held tight and rolled his hand over forcefully, exposing the inside of his forearm and the bold, black letters of the word *Bonnie*.

"Care to explain this now?" she asked as she traced the marked skin with her fingertip.

He gathered his wits, took a deep breath, and assumed his storytelling voice. "Well, once upon a time, I broke into the town library after hours with my girlfriend, and we spent the rest of the night hiding from the cops. From then on, our friends thought it would be funny to call us Bonnie and Clyde every time a cop came around." He shrugged his shoulder in acceptance. "Not my finest moment."

"What an interesting story. Why did you break into the library?" she asked in fake inquiry as she continued to trace the tattoo.

"Why *did* we break into the library? We didn't actually take anything, did we?"

She sighed because *she* remembered exactly what happened. He was right, it wasn't their finest moment. In fact, she still regretted the act to this day. She'd never done anything so reckless in her life before or since. "At the time, I blamed it all on Ms. Berkenstein."

His eyebrow rose in question. "Elaborate."

"The librarian. She had it out for me and refused to let me fact check *one little thing* for my research paper in the reference section at school because I was 'too loud' that one time. She said if I thought I was too good to follow the rules of the library then she didn't have to follow them either and allow me access."

"Oh yeah. I remember now. She was pretty strict about her library."

Her fingertip ministrations moved to the palm of his hand without pausing. The callouses felt old and deep, but she didn't skip around them.

"So I wanted to prove that I didn't need her to finish my paper. You suggested breaking into the town library and just find what I needed and leave."

"Ahh. It's all coming back to me now. That was one of the worst ideas I ever had. You probably shouldn't listen to me or my ideas." He shook his head. "I remember hiding in bushes all over town that night running from the cops. And I remember having to turn ourselves in the next morning when our parents found out."

She could feel her cheeks turning red at the memory. His hand clamped around hers, holding her in place, even though she hadn't attempted to move.

"I'm sorry I got you into that. I knew it was wrong, and I was old enough to know better."

She'd made her peace with the event. She'd apologized to her parents and the city police. She even apologized to Ms. Berkenstein, and that was one of the hardest and biggest learning experiences of her life. Asking God for forgiveness had been easy. She knew she'd done wrong, and she regretted it. Taking her failures to God had been crucial.

"Dakota, I'm not mad at you. It wasn't all your fault. I made the decision same as you, and we both apologized and asked for forgiveness. Let's put it behind us."

He nodded. "I can do that." To diffuse the tension, he gave her a sly wink.

"When did you get it?" she asked. She knew he would understand she meant the tattoo. It must have been after she left.

One heartbeat passed before he seemed to decide to face the truth. "Right before the last time I went to New York."

She was confused. "You mean you had this that night we broke up, and you didn't tell me?"

"It wasn't a good time," he pointed out, and his brows drew closer, casting shadows over his eyes. "Not to mention it was another one of my stupid ideas. I've done some crazy things in my life. I'm nowhere near perfect, but getting a woman's nickname tattooed on my arm wasn't my finest moment."

She gave a single laugh and nodded her agreement. "You mean you did something crazier than getting a tattoo?"

He was quiet, and she knew he was thinking about something he didn't intend to share with her. "It's just an example of how I tried to take things into my own hands. Things I couldn't control. I should've prayed about what was going on in our relationship more, instead of running out and permanently marking your name on my skin. I should have tried to understand why we were drifting apart. I should have asked God about His plan, not mine."

She could see the regret in his eyes, and it was like looking in a mirror. "Fair enough." She watched a couple in the booth beside them gathering up their trash and belongings while strapping a sleeping infant into his carrier. "If it makes you feel any better, I made the same mistake."

His brows drew together. "What do you mean?"

"I got a tattoo too."

His eyes opened wide and his mouth opened and closed without speaking.

"When I was in New York, I was out with some friends and they decided it would be fun to get a tattoo. You know I always said I wouldn't get one, but I was pressured. I was with new people, and I didn't have many friends. I just wanted to fit in."

He looked down at their linked hands and said, "That's a... surprise."

"I know. It's not like me, and I regret it. I didn't want to do it, but I was scared. It's one of the many reminders I have that I wasn't made for the city."

He rubbed the back of his neck and asked, "What is it, if you don't mind me asking?"

She smiled. "You'll laugh."

He squeezed her hand. "I promise not to laugh."

She took a deep breath and said, "It's an apple and a peach."

When he looked confused, she explained, "It's half an apple and half a peach. The big apple and a Georgia peach."

"You're kidding."

She shook her head. "Nope. My heart was divided when I was in New York. I loved the city, but my home was a small, Georgia town."

He released her hand and stood with the red tray that contained their trash. "Come on. I have a surprise for you, and I can't wait any longer."

"A surprise? When did you have time to get me a surprise?" She'd been with him at lunch yesterday, and he'd fished with Tyler until after dark.

His steps faltered and he began to laugh—a full, hearty laugh that couldn't be contained. When he nearly dropped the tray, she looked around to find the other patrons watching them.

"What's so funny?"

"You'll think it's funny too when you find out how much time I had to get this surprise for you."

The suspense was eating at her insides, and his knowing smirk was beginning to irritate her. He was driving five miles per hour below the speed limit, and he had to know it was a true test of her patience to keep her mouth shut.

She didn't handle surprises well. She was impatient, and waiting for surprises was difficult. She needed to take her mind off it.

"So, tell me about what you've been up to lately." She leaned toward him from her seat in the truck and poked his arm. "Looks like you've been working out."

He rolled his eyes but kept his attention on the road ahead. "I don't work out often. This is just part of the job. I stay busy."

"What is your job?" she asked. Sissy said he was in construction, so she assumed road construction. After all, she'd almost made a speed bump out of him with her car at the beginning of the week.

"Which one?" he smiled. "I have a few. I don't let myself get bored, so I try to fill all hours of the day."

"You work multiple jobs?"

"Yeah, it keeps my mind and body busy. Declan and I build houses together. I work part-time in road construction, and I take on odd jobs around town when I'm not doing either of those. If I don't stop, I..." he dropped the sentence like nothing had happened.

"You what?" she asked tentatively.

"We're almost there." He was trying to divert her, so she would let it slide. If he wanted to tell her, he would.

She looked up to see where they were.

"Are we going to the barn?" she asked. They were close to the dirt road that led to the barn... and the field where she found him drunk two days ago.

"No. Not the barn."

Before they reached the road to the barn, he turned onto a gravel path that hadn't existed six years ago when she left. Her anxiety morphed into serenity as the blood of the earth surrounded them. The dense trees insulated them in warmth from a hidden sun that couldn't penetrate the canopy of gently dying leaves.

Then the scene changed without warning and the forest gave way to a sprawling meadow. The field before her was a stunning gift to behold. She'd grown used to the comforting insulation of the forest and for some reason had expected it to continue indefinitely. The open area before her was picturesque, and despite her mind's protest at the departure of the woods, she didn't feel exposed. She felt wholly welcome and complete in the wake of its surprising arrival.

He stopped on the edge of the tree line and put the truck in park.

"Where are we?" she asked as she turned quickly in all directions, trying to place herself. Surely, they were close to the land the barn and pond sat on, but she hadn't seen this place before. She thought they'd explored every inch of Dakota's family land.

"I bought the land adjacent to my family's property. When I saw this place, I couldn't pass it up."

"When?" Dakota's family had sprawling acres of beautiful land. Why would he need more?

He looked at her like she should know the answer. "About a month before we broke up."

Her heart beat double time, and her mouth refused to form words.

His smile broke free and he said, "I told you I had plenty of time to get this surprise for you. You were just supposed to get it six years ago." He chuckled and turned to resume driving.

He drove slowly, allowing her to orient herself to the new place. It was the most beautiful land she'd ever seen. She couldn't have found a more picturesque meadow in a *National Geographic* magazine.

"Your family owns so much land. Why did you want to buy this too?" She had to ask because she couldn't quite understand his actions.

"I needed a place that was *ours*. Something that didn't belong to my old family, but our new family."

Well, that certainly felt like a commitment. She'd been uprooting her life, and consequently, his too, six years ago. He'd been digging himself in for the long haul. Now, she knew she'd made the right decision when she hadn't let him come with her to New York.

As if he could read her thoughts, he said, "I didn't expect this to make you stay, but I wanted you to always have a place to come home to."

A few seconds later, they rounded a corner and a pristine farmhouse came into view. It looked new, but it sat nestled into the land as if it had always belonged. She drew in an audible gasp and leaned forward, bracing her hands on the dashboard of the truck. He pulled the truck to a stop in front of the house, and she still didn't move.

Her eyes pricked and her nose tingled. She was able to close her mouth to find she needed to swallow, but a lump formed in her throat.

"What is this?" she whispered. Her words barely held volume as her eyes filled with tears.

"This is home."

She couldn't yet understand how she was looking at a house that had only existed in her dreams. It looked so much like the one she and Sissy had described in detail as teenagers creating fantasies of enormous proportions. He'd either listened to their ramblings *very carefully,* or Sissy's hands had been in this.

How had this happened without her knowledge? He'd made her silly childish dreams a reality *after* she'd broken his heart.

She turned to him and let the tears fall. "I can't believe I missed it."

He smiled. "You missed the hard part, and you get to enjoy the finished product."

She sobbed at the realization. Did she really get to enjoy it? She would be here two more days, but he would always be here living in her dream home, living the life they were meant to have lived together. Her heart broke for all she'd lost. It was right in front of her, the life she'd cast aside.

"This is..." She wiped her eyes hurriedly. "A huge surprise." Her emotions were mixed. This surprise felt bittersweet. "I can't believe you built it. I didn't think you even cared about the house."

"Of course, I cared." He pulled her to him in a hug. "It was my job as your boyfriend to make sure you got all the things you wanted... even when you weren't around to tell me what those wants were anymore. Trust me, you and Sissy talked enough about this house that I had plenty of material to go on." He brushed her hair gently from her face as she cried silent tears.

"Actually, this house led me to my job. This was the first house I built, and I learned a lot while doing it." She leaned back to look at him. "Sissy explained a lot of the design terms I didn't understand, and Brian and Ian helped me get my hands on the parts and materials I needed. They own the only hardware store in town. All of our friends helped out on their days off. I usually always had at least one person here to help."

She could see it all so clearly now.

"It started as a way to keep my mind off of you. I wanted to *avoid* memories of you, and I kept my mind busy by building a house. I couldn't talk about you or anything we used to do together. I just decided to build a house because, even though it had been *our* plan, I couldn't let it go. It still felt like the plan. I didn't realize what I'd done until it was finished, and by that time, it was home."

She was sobbing again. She couldn't bear to hear about the hurt she'd put him through. "I'm sorry. I'm so sorry."

"There's nothing to be sorry about." He took her chin in his hand and demanded she look at him. "I wanted to come home to you every night more than anything in this world. I made every decision about this house in a daze that revolved around missing you. I created a home for you, whether I liked it or not."

"Dakota..."

He didn't wait for her to finish. He bounded out of the truck and jogged to her door. His hand was offered to her before the door was fully opened.

"So, are you ready to come home now?"

CHAPTER 16
Dakota

His heart thudded a quick rhythm as he led her up the stained, wooden steps leading to the wraparound porch. White columns served as dividers between draping ferns that hung around the perimeter.

When the hard soles of his boots met the sturdy boards of the porch, he waited for her to reach him before he took her shoulders and turned her to face the way they'd just come.

Dakota didn't have to see her face to know she would appreciate this view. From the moment he stood on this plot of land, he knew this was the scene he wanted to see every day. He hadn't been able to completely understand it at the time because everything had been shadowed and gray, but now he knew what had captured his heart to this exact spot.

He'd thought of Lindsey when he saw it. The hills had been glowing verdant, the trees as dark as the rind of an avocado. And the day he first stood on this spot, the sky had been a vast and endless ocean of blue, just as it was today. Now, the leaves were beginning to change with the season, and he recalled the added excitement he'd felt after realizing autumn was just as beautiful as spring and summer here.

Dakota knew Lindsey would love it, and he'd grabbed onto something that would unite them again.

Her head slowly turned in all directions, taking in the landscape surrounding them. When she'd taken her fill of the scenery, she slowly walked the length of the porch, dragging her fingertips along the railing. She reached the corner while he held his ground and gave her space.

When she returned, her arms were crossed over her chest, but she still strode evenly without giving away her assessment. He drew labored breaths as he waited for her to speak.

She stopped only a few inches from him and placed both of her hands on his chest. "This place. It's so beautiful."

"We're not finished yet." He grabbed her hand and walked backward toward the front door. She followed him, and their eyes never wavered from each other.

He stopped at the navy-blue door that led into the house. When he'd told Sissy he wasn't putting a blue door on his house, she assured him it would "make the whole house pop." Now, as he gripped the knob of the blue door, he knew she'd been right. He'd thought it would look ridiculous, but Sissy had seen something he hadn't until the door was on the hinges.

After wondering what could've possessed Lindsey and Sissy to decide on a dark-blue door, he finally figured it out when he looked at the front of the house. The color of that door couldn't be found naturally anywhere you looked around this house. It'd been Lindsey's way of making sure she added her own touch to nature. The best part was the way the door stood out against the white walls of the house but didn't demand attention. It merely blended in its own way.

Lindsey looked from him to the door and smiled knowingly.

He sighed. "You weren't even here and you won the battle of the door. For the record, I thought it was crazy."

"And..." she prompted with tears still hanging in her eyes.

"And I was wrong." He rolled his eyes and smiled at their playful banter. She made him so happy he could hardly stand it.

"Are you ready to see the rest?"

"I don't know." Her face fell into concern. "I'm scared," she whispered.

"Of what?" he asked.

"I'm scared I'll love it," she whispered.

On that note, he opened the door and led her inside.

Lindsey

She was still in shock and unsure what to expect as she followed him through the beautiful front door.

The interior was stunning. A perfect farmhouse with all the comforts of home.

She couldn't speak, so she let her attention fall on various things in the room. The soft gray couch was pillowy and large. Of course, a man as broad and tall as Dakota would need larger-than-life furniture.

He stepped farther into the room, but she didn't have the courage to look at him yet. She ran her fingers along a wooden table that sat against the wall adjacent to the door. The wood was worn, but she could tell great pains had been taken in the sanding and construction. The top was as smooth as glass.

"Brian made it. He builds furniture on the side. Actually, only a few pieces of furniture in the whole house came from a store."

She should've known. Their old friend Brian had always been a handyman. There wasn't much he couldn't make on his own. And Dakota never did anything halfway. He would've had his hand in every crack and crevice of this place.

"He's very talented. Did you make any of it?" She still couldn't bring herself to look at him.

"I did. I built the table in the kitchen and the master bed."

Not only was this place his home, but he'd made himself a part of every single thing inside of it. The house had bits and pieces of him everywhere. She could see his signature written on the walls.

She looked for decorations and felt a pang at the idea that another woman may have enjoyed this place in her absence. Still, she didn't find many feminine touches. The house itself wasn't particularly manly, but there were few wall furnishings and no photographs at all.

He stood in one place with his arms crossed over his chest as she surveyed the house. She found the hand-carved, dark hardwood floors she'd mentioned once. They'd visited the local country club for a wedding, and she'd fallen in love with the flooring. Now, it lined the dining room and hallway of his home. The dining room ceiling housed a medallion larger than her arm span in the center reminiscent of colonial homes in the area.

When she finished perusing the common areas, she realized she was more afraid of seeing the rest of the house than facing him. She turned to him but didn't take a step. She felt selfish, but the things he'd accomplished without her stung her pride and her heart.

"I don't know what to say. It looks like you've created a wonderful life." Tears threatened to spill again, but she held them back.

He approached her in two long strides, and she felt utterly afraid of whatever may come next.

He stared at her, dared her to move. "You said I would find someone else."

Why was he bringing that up? Was he trying to

hurt her? Had she not apologized enough for the wrongs she'd done to him? "Stop. I said I'm—"

"You were wrong. You were the only one. You were the one that got away." He grabbed her arms and nearly shook her in his effort to gain her full attention, to make her understand. His bright-blue eyes were inches from hers, and his smell—leather and a hint of fresh earth, just as she remembered—permeated her nose. "You made it impossible to fight for you and just as impossible to give up. I've been stuck in a half-life."

She didn't know what to say as his hands brushed the bare skin of her arms and climbed up across her shoulders. His palms rested on each side of her neck and his fingers snaked into the hair at the nape. If breathing had been difficult before, it was impossible now.

Her hands came to rest on his broad chest. He was so warm, and she wanted to melt into the safe haven he promised.

She wanted so many things that were so far from her grasp. She wanted things she couldn't dare hope to have... all with him.

How could she have walked away from this? Nothing compared to the way Dakota made her feel. Nothing came close to how much she loved him. How had she broken something so precious and amazing? How had she drifted so far from her home?

She buried her face in his neck and clung to him. She wanted to keep him. She wanted to stop time and remain stagnant in this moment surrounded by him.

"I'm sorry... for the way I acted last time we kissed. You deserve so much better." He cradled her head in one hand and rubbed her back with the other.

"Shh. Let's not talk about the past. Just be here with me."

"It's hard to believe we're here—that you're here. I dream about this every night."

This was her home, her grounding place. She belonged in Dakota's arms.

"Lindz..."

His voice was pained, and she cut him off. "Shh. I'm here now." She stroked his hair as she fought the tears of regret. When she could no longer contain her emotions, she moved to wipe them away.

He caught her hand before she could discard any of her embarrassing tears. "No. Don't hide."

He kissed the tears on her cheeks and pulled back to look at her.

He was the most beautiful man she'd ever laid eyes on. Mostly because he was good inside and out. She knew men weren't usually described as beautiful, and he was certainly ruggedly handsome, but the complete package that was Dakota's heart was inherently good.

His jaw was sharp, his shoulders were broad, his skin was tan, and those eyes. His pale eyes against his dark skin were entrancing. The way he moved was full of masculinity, but the way he held her was soft and tender. Each of the things she loved about him were fascinating on their own. Together they were a force to be reckoned with.

"I love it when you cry when you're happy. I didn't understand it at first, and I worried. Now, things are a little clearer. I think it means you're really here. With me."

He did understand. She was consumed by him and their love, and the rush of emotion was too much to contain. He hadn't meant physically here with him. He meant emotionally.

"That's exactly what it means."

She studied his face and noticed the scar that ran a jagged line through his eyebrow. She touched it, and he flinched.

"I'm sorry. Does it hurt?"

"No," was his clipped answer.

"Will you tell me what happened?" she asked tentatively.

His body was tense, and his eyes almost seemed scared. He released a deep breath and answered. "All right, but let's talk about it over dinner."

CHAPTER 17

Lindsey

Lindsey sat on the back porch railing while he placed steaks on the grill for their dinner.

It made her a little nervous when he put off her question about the scar on his head, and now her anxiety was threatening to tumble into overdrive. She took a deep breath to calm her nerves just as the smoke from the grill consumed her in a fog. She coughed and waved a hand in front of her face before jumping down onto her bare feet.

"Sorry, Lindz. You know smoke follows beauty."

If he was making jokes, maybe whatever he had to tell her wasn't so bad.

He closed the grill, picked up his soda, and turned to face her, leaning against the porch railing. "I'm gonna need you to keep it together during this story. It's ancient history, and I don't like it one bit. Okay?" His tone was serious, and she nodded in agreement, scared to speak.

"I had a hard time after you left. I didn't know what I was gonna do with my life without you, my best friend, and I didn't have much going for me. Every time I would remember you, I would drink to forget you. Needless to say, I was always drinking."

He hung his head and linked his fingers behind his neck for a moment before throwing his hands down in fists. The muscles of his shoulders tensed and relaxed.

"I wrecked the Bronco one night. I was drunk. And I almost died."

"What? When?" She had to piece this together. It didn't make sense. Sissy wouldn't have been able to keep it from her. Her throat constricted, and her eyes stung. How had she not known?

"Almost a year after you left."

She couldn't help the catch in her words now. "Why didn't someone tell me?"

"I asked everyone to keep you out of it. I didn't want you to see me like that, and I was ashamed of myself."

"I don't think that was fair to me, Dakota." Her voice was rising with her panic as she stabbed a finger into her chest.

"I didn't mean to intentionally hurt myself. I wasn't at my best, and I think my mind and body were in agreement that the way I was living wasn't going to cut it much longer. I sort of gave up one night."

She turned away from him and shielded her body with her arms. Her Dakota had been close to death and no one had told her. She couldn't imagine the pain she would live in if she couldn't see him again. She couldn't imagine the heartache he must have endured to end up where he did.

"I don't remember much, but I was conscious long enough to call Declan. He was stationed in Texas, so I knew he wasn't a lifeline. I just felt like I needed to talk to someone who cared for a minute before I died."

She cried silent tears that burned her chest and throat as he spoke. She cursed herself for not being here for him, for letting him lie in a ditch half dead and longing for someone who cared.

"Declan called Sissy and she called the police. They searched for me. I don't know how long I was there, but they had half the county out looking for me. Sissy found me, but she won't talk about it. Honestly, I understand because I don't like talking about it either. No one around here will let me live it down. I couldn't act right, and I messed up."

She turned back to him when her anger got the best of her. "You could've *died*, Dakota. You could've killed someone else." She paced a short line in her fury. "Why didn't Sissy tell me?" She was seething and shaking from the adrenaline.

"I told you. I asked her not to."

"But why would you do that?"

The phone in his pocket beeped, and he ignored it. He crossed his arms and leaned back against the railing. "Please explain to me how things would've gone down if you'd gotten that call. I'll wait."

Without stopping to think, she screamed, "I would've come back!"

"Uh-huh. I'm guessing you were right in the middle of auditions or booked shows, and you would've resented the intrusion. I wanted you back more than I wanted to breathe, but I never wanted you to come back because you felt obligated."

Her anger died, and she strode to him purposefully and latched herself onto him. How could he think so little of her? In all the years they'd been separated, she never stopped loving him. Her arms wound around him, and she buried her face in his neck. She clung to him as hard as she possibly could. Her irrational mind was warped by the idea that she could still lose him if she gave an inch between them.

He wrapped her in his arms, and she willed herself to sink into him, to become linked to whatever it was that constituted the whole, living man that she held. After a moment, his phone buzzed again, shattering the stillness between them.

"I can't lose you, Dakota. You're too important to me," she whispered. He felt more than just important. He felt vital to her happiness.

"I've always been yours, Lindz."

Those words broke something in her heart, and she couldn't live in a world where she held back from the things that mattered most to her. What was the point?

"I love you." She didn't whisper. Her voice was steady and sure. She wanted him to hear her loud and clear.

He pulled her away so he could see her face. "I never stopped loving you. Just promise me you won't treat me differently because of what I did. I won't make the same mistake again."

"Dakota, I need you to trust me. Trust me to be able to help you if you feel like the problem could come back. If I can't help you, trust that I'll find someone who can."

She could see the wound inside him as she realized the problem *was* back. She was the disturbance that carried his addiction, and he couldn't seem to fight the darkness she carried.

"What happened this week?" she asked.

"I'm not an alcoholic. I know that sounds like denial, but I can go out with the boys and stop after one drink. I can go days and weeks or months without even thinking about it. I don't crave it or need it... until I want it to numb me."

He was still holding her, and she linked her fingers behind his neck and placed their foreheads together the way she used to say good-bye to him when they were young. They never said the words. She just pulled him close by the nape, and they made a silent promise to see each other again soon. Still to this day, they'd never said good-bye to each other.

"I know this is easier said than done, but what would it take to make sure you never do that again?"

He held her tight and whispered, "I can promise you now it'll never happen again." Dakota had always been brutally honest. He would never make a promise he couldn't keep.

"How can you say that?" She wasn't accusing him of dishonesty. She just wanted to know how it'd been so simple to promise something so enormous.

"I just know I won't. I've got my eye on the prize, and I'm not letting anything stand in my way."

She blushed and hope bloomed in her chest as she thought he might mean her. Truth be told, he didn't have to win her over. She was already head over heels.

"I'm serious, Lindz. You're it, and I'm not letting you walk away this time."

His phone beeped again, and he pulled it from his pocket and frowned before replacing it without responding. He pulled away from her and said, "Let me check on the steaks. I'm not about to serve you jerky for dinner."

She stepped back and gave him room to man the grill.

Her worlds were crashing together fast, and she needed to make some big decisions. Sure, she was happy here. She was happier than she'd been since she left this place. In some ways, it still felt like a vacation. You were supposed to enjoy your trip and wish you could never leave, but reality dictated you return to the monotonous real world and continue your job and boring life.

It felt like a huge leap to uproot her life, but would it really be that difficult? She didn't own much, and she didn't have anything tying her to North Carolina, except a lease and a job.

Her heart constricted as she thought of being in between jobs again. She'd hated that part about the entertainment industry, and she didn't look forward to job hunting again. Not to mention the moving expenses.

Twilight blanketed the field as Dakota strode toward her and grabbed her hand severing her stressful thoughts.

"Dinner is ready."

CHAPTER 18
Lindey

They ate in silence, and her lighter mood was gradually returning. Dakota didn't need a reason to reach for her hand or kiss her palm between bites.

Neither wanted to let the peaceful moment pass. Facing the uncertainty of what may come next meant possibly living a life without any more of this, and that didn't seem like an option anymore.

When they finished eating, Dakota grabbed their plates and hastily threw them in the sink. "Come on." He extended his hand to her, and she took it. "You need to see the rest of our home."

She stood on shaky feet as he led her by the hand into a hallway dimmed by the fading sun. He stopped at the first door on the right and turned to her. "This will be the master bedroom."

Lindsey's head tilted slightly as she asked, "Will be?"

His gaze was focused on anything except her as he admitted, "I don't sleep in the master bedroom. It didn't feel right when I moved in. That was supposed to be our room as man and wife. I chose one of the guest bedrooms and made it my own for now."

He gripped her hand tighter in his and finally met her gaze. "If you decide to stay—if you decide to be with me—this will be our room when we're married."

Without waiting for her reaction, he turned the doorknob and led her into the room.

She stopped in the doorway, overwhelmed by the scene that lay before her. It was just like she imagined. The walls were the color of driftwood and the mahogany furniture stood out against the light of the walls. Heather-gray curtains hung from floor to ceiling around a large window overlooking the front yard and the dark rolling hills beyond.

Her attention turned to the bed—the piece Dakota claimed to have made himself. The posts were thick and hand carved in a rough manner that made the bed seem to still have its foot in the ground from which it once grew.

She turned to him and smiled. "I can't believe you did all of this." She took in the doorframes, the ceiling, and the crown molding. "It looks like…"

"Does it look like what you wanted?" His weight shifted slowly from side to side as he waited for her reaction.

She shook her head and laughed. "It looks better than I imagined."

He crossed his arms and nodded. "Sissy's good at her job, and it sure helped that she knows you like the back of her hand."

She crossed the room to stand before him, looking up into his stained-glass eyes. "You've done so much. You've been working so hard." She released a huff and looked around. "You have so much to show for your time and effort."

The hollow feeling she carried weighed heavy in her heart. She was the one who ran away chasing something she couldn't touch. She was the one who would come crawling home with nothing but wasted years to show for it.

"Hey." Dakota's hand cupped her chin and turned her to face him. "Stop."

"Stop what?"

"I know what you're thinking. You haven't failed at anything. So what if you're not acting anymore? You tried. Just because it didn't work out doesn't mean you failed. It means that wasn't God's plan for you. It wasn't your path. That means He has a better plan for you."

She leaned into his embrace and gave a single nod. Maybe he did know what it was like to fail. Maybe he was the only person who knew how unworthy she felt.

He held her in his comforting arms for a moment before pulling away. "Let's see the rest of the house."

She followed him through guest rooms, bathrooms, closets, a garage, and what could only be considered a man cave in the basement before they made their way back to the main floor. Dakota did so much more than simply build a house. He'd created a home from scratch and her imagination. She rubbed her hands up and down her bare arms as she thought about her minimally furnished apartment in North Carolina.

Dakota startled her from her thoughts when he appeared before her holding out a coat that was more than a few sizes too large. "Here. You'll need this."

She slipped her arms into the sleeves and let the coat swallow her small frame. Dakota's natural scent of wood and dirt wafted around her, and she leaned toward her shoulder to capture the smell. This was the aroma that accompanied the memories of her teenage years. The best times of her life had been surrounded by Dakota's scent.

He led her through the rooms toward the back of the house, turning off the lights as he went. When he reached the back door, he gestured for her to lead the way onto the porch where they grilled earlier.

She realized his intention as soon as she stepped outside. The cloudless sky was sprinkled with dim stars overshadowed by a blinding full moon. She shook her head at the amazing sight.

"I forgot about the moon." It sounded impossible, but it'd been ages since she'd admired the beauty of the heavens.

He stepped behind her and wrapped her in his embrace. "How could you forget this?"

She hadn't forgotten really. She'd protected her

fragile heart from remembering the things she'd stolen from herself.

"You know, the lights of New York City are beautiful, but these lights..." Her voice dipped with reverence at the stars and the imposing moon. "These are God's lights."

Seeing the beauty of this place, the kindness of the man beside her, and pouring over the memories that made her into the woman she was today was too much to take in at once.

She was fortunate beyond measure, but she felt trapped at the same time. Of all the wonderful things that stood before her—the stars, Dakota, home—none of them seemed attainable. This place wasn't her home, this man wasn't her boyfriend anymore, and those memories were useless when she didn't have a connection to the people in them any longer.

The loss that hit her the hardest was God, but she was the only one to blame. She turned her back on Him all those years ago, chasing a worldly dream. She'd shunned Him and hidden ever since, and yet He still chose to let her have these moments of beauty. God still cared for her. He still protected her and loved her.

But just like the man standing here with her, she'd turned her back on Him years ago, and she was afraid to face Him again. When would she be strong enough to take responsibility for what she'd done? Was coming home to this place or her Heavenly Father even possible? She'd made so many mistakes, and her pride hurt. Most of all, her heart ached for the love she hadn't known in a long time. Would she ever be able to enjoy love without making excuses?

"Dakota, you told me you're not the same man I knew back then." She felt his arms stiffen around her, but he didn't deny it. "Well, I'm not the same either. I've changed."

"You're still the same, Lindz."

"No, I'm not, and they haven't all been good changes. I've been... lost."

"What do you mean?"

"I—I drifted away from God. I forgot Him, and now I'm ashamed."

Dakota's cheek rested on her head. "It's all right, Lindz. I know better than anyone that mistakes can be forgiven and the vices that rule us can be tamed. I pray for help all the time, and it usually comes after I've had to pray for forgiveness. I know now that my mistake was putting my faith in the substance instead of God. It only made my problem worse."

He was right. She just had to humble herself before God.

"Repent. That's what I've been told many times by people who were trying to help me in my darkest time. But the best advice I heard was to ask for help. I had to learn that making the same mistakes and asking for forgiveness wasn't doing any good if I wasn't trying to make myself better. When I stopped running and changed the things I was doing, I realized I didn't have to ask forgiveness for quite so many things."

She smiled and pulled away from him. "You

were wrong." The moonlight illuminated his face, and she knew every curve and expression written there in the starlight. "You are the same man I used to know."

Dakota was still that same man who promised to love her until their last days. He was the same man who swore to be the spiritual leader of their family. He was still that man who would do and say what was best for her.

He gave a nod so tiny she almost missed it. "I want to be good for you. There are so many ways that I don't feel good enough for you, but I can promise you I'll keep trying my best to be the best man I can be for you."

He held her face in his hands, the callouses brushing against her fair skin, and leaned closer. "Lindsey, I love you. I'll always love you."

And then he kissed her. Time was suspended, and the air around them paused as his lips touched hers. Warmth flooded her bones as tears sprang to her eyes. She closed them to contain the emotion, but her heart was too far gone.

The kiss was short and sweet, but she would be forever changed. She was stronger, and she couldn't imagine a life without him anymore. Her heart beat double-time, reminiscent of her first kiss—their first kiss.

She smiled, thankful to know that not only was Dakota working on himself every day, but she would be fighting right alongside him to be a better version of herself. She felt as if she could do anything, knowing Dakota supported her.

She stood and wrapped Dakota's coat more snugly around her shoulders. "I have to get back to Sissy's soon. I promised her I would get up with Lydia tonight."

Dakota followed her inside. "Let me take over baby duty tonight. Sissy has a daybed in the nursery I can sleep on, and everyone can rest tonight."

She gave a short laugh and turned to him. "Since when do you know how to take care of a baby?"

"I don't, but you can fill me in on the midnight duties on the way there. Plus, I'd like to spend some more time with Lydia. I took off work this week to help Sissy and see more of the baby, but I've spent most of the week with you. As much as I've enjoyed our time together, I'm missing out on baby snuggles."

Lindsey pulled his coat off her shoulders. "You really are smitten with Lydia."

"Of course," he said as he settled the coat back around her. "I'm really excited about being an uncle. I love kids. I spend a lot of time with Marcus' brothers. Sometimes, Marcus needs help, but sometimes Megan just needs a break."

It'd been so long since she thought about Marcus and his siblings. "Poor Megan. She must be a teenager now, and it can't be easy having so many brothers."

Dakota shook his head. "Sometimes, I wonder how much longer she'll keep her sanity with those boys. She needs a mom."

Their friend Marcus raised his siblings on his own. Their mother had all but succumbed to drugs and neglected her many children.

"That's awful. Is their mother still…"

"She's still alive. Barely."

Her heart broke thinking of the daunting task Marcus had taken on to save his family. She couldn't understand how some children, like Lydia, had more than enough people to love them, while some children were lucky to have anyone at all to care for them.

"Let's go. Sissy will be worried about you."

CHAPTER 19
Dakota

Dakota was jerked from sleep by a wail that sent his heart pounding in panic. Fueled by adrenaline, he looked around the room, letting his eyesight adjust to the darkness to see a squirming Lydia in the crib across the room.

He took a deep breath with the understanding and rubbed his eyes as Lindsey stuck her head into the room. "I'll be right back with the bottle."

So much for letting Lindsey sleep. She'd filled him in on Lydia's nightly routine on the drive over, and he'd assured her he was capable of heating up a bottle of milk just how she taught him.

He stood and saw the red digital numbers of the clock beside him that read 1:13 AM. Lydia had silenced her wail for the moment, but she was squirming as if the time to fully wake was drawing closer. Stretching his arms above his head, he followed Lindsey down the stairs and into the kitchen.

"I'm coming too. You can show me what to do so I can help next time."

"Okay." She removed a bottle from the refrigerator and placed it in a pod that resembled a mini spaceship.

He rubbed his hands over his face vigorously. "Walk me through this. What's with the chemistry lab contraption?"

She yawned as she pressed a couple of buttons on the machine and turned to him. He could barely discern her smile in the dark kitchen.

"It's a bottle warmer, and it just speeds this up. Cold milk could give her an upset tummy, so we warm it up a bit. This takes care of it in a couple of minutes versus the fifteen it takes when you run it under hot water."

"Got it... I think." He was still half asleep, and taking notes was the last thing he wanted to do.

"I'm going to the nursery. Bring the bottle when it beeps." She rubbed his shoulder as she passed and the part of him that wasn't screaming to go back to sleep was wallowing in the domesticity of this midnight hour with Lindsey.

In their years together before she left, he'd assumed they would face everything in life together. He thought they would get married, have kids, and grow old together. He'd never really thought about the finer points of those broad topics, but he recognized this as a glimpse at what he and Lindsey might've been doing if their family had come to fruition.

When the machine beeped, he took the bottle and

made his way to the nursery. He found Lindsey pacing and gently bouncing a whining, wiggling Lydia. He held the bottle out to Lindsey, and she asked, "Do you want to feed her?"

He hesitated, but he was too intrigued not to accept. He nodded and she motioned to the rocking chair. He sat and Lindsey gently placed the baby in his arms.

Tilting her slightly, he asked, "Is this right?"

Lindsey positioned the baby at a steeper angle and motioned for him to go ahead with the bottle. "We're practicing paced feeding since Sissy is breastfeeding, but I won't bore you with the specifics. I'll just walk you through it."

"Perfect." Even the specifics of the angle felt a little overwhelming. "Is it just a natural thing for women to know how to care for babies, or is it an acquired skill?"

She laughed. "I knew less than nothing about taking care of a baby before this week. I've been listening and learning as I go, but I guess that's what it's always like in the beginning. You learn through experience."

Shadows covered Lindsey's face from the nightlight in the corner, but he couldn't help staring at her as she propped her back against the crib. She would make an amazing mother.

The nursery was silent as Lydia drank her milk, and a sense of peace fell over him.

"Did you ever think you'd be sitting in a nursery in

the middle of the night rocking a baby to sleep with me?" he couldn't help but ask.

"I did... at one point. After we broke up, it was hard to think about things like that. Honestly, this isn't an accurate representation of parenthood. It's an unwritten rule that both parents are not up in the middle of the night with the baby." She propped her hands on the crib rail behind her as they talked.

He forced his gaze to Lydia and softly kissed the dark tuft of her hair. She was so small and innocent. She was a clean slate with no regrets, no mistakes, and endless possibilities ahead.

"This isn't real, Kota. Being a parent is tough. Caring for Lydia isn't all roses. Even the carefree Sissy and the well-educated Tyler have been frazzled this week."

She knelt before him on the carpet and removed the almost empty bottle from the sleeping Lydia's mouth.

"But I swear it's all worth it. I've been a bystander caught in a rush of extremes this week, but I've never been happier than I am here with the people I love. It's completely humbling."

"Do you want a family, Lindz?" The question came to him suddenly and slightly uninvited, but now that his fear had been exposed to the air, he couldn't bring himself to regret the asking.

She stroked Lydia's hair and didn't look at him as she answered, "I do. Meeting Lydia just wrote my decision in stone. I love her more than I thought possible, and she isn't even mine."

That was what he wanted to hear, and he released a content breath.

"Can I put her in the crib now?" he whispered.

She moved to make room for him to place the sleeping baby in the crib, and he caught himself again marveling at the beauty of a newborn.

When he turned, Lindsey stretched her hand to him. He pulled her close and kissed her head. "Good night."

"Good night."

Dakota stood in the quiet nursery and watched her go. He wanted to grab her and demand she stay in Carson, beg her to see the life he could give her. He wanted his panic to be eased, but the serenity of the night called for whispers and muffled footsteps down the hallway.

When he returned to bed, he prayed again that he wouldn't wake up in the morning to find Lindsey had all been a dream.

They spent the next day taking orders from Sissy who was cementing her role as a new mother. Luckily, she mostly asked them to watch Lydia so she could take care of chores around the house.

Spending the day watching Lydia sleep was a walk in the park. Granted, he just waited for Lindsey to tell him what to do. She sent him to search for gas drops and find Sissy when it was time for Lydia to eat. Mostly, they watched the Lifetime movies and soap operas Sissy had become obsessed with while he rocked Lydia's bassinet with his foot.

Spending a lazy day with Lindsey turned out to be a welcome change of pace. He knew with growing certainty that this was what he wanted, and he wanted it with her. A blissful Saturday on the couch with her was the stuff his dreams were made of these days.

Sissy finally entered the living area around 4:00 PM rubbing a towel over her wet hair. "You will never understand how amazing a shower feels until you haven't had one in days and you're covered in every type of baby fluid that exists." She shook with a chill and plopped into the recliner, arms and legs sprawling.

"Y'all are free to go, by the way," Sissy added as an afterthought.

He turned to Lindsey who was spread out over the couch beside him with her legs resting across his lap. "Can I take you out on the town tonight?" He gave her a playful grin.

"Like a date?" Her face lit up as she asked.

"Not *like* a date. Definitely a date." He wasn't beating around the bush anymore.

"Can we go to Rusty's? Wait, is Rusty's still open?"

"Of course. That place isn't going anywhere. Plus, Brian and Addie are playing tonight." He leaned over to kiss Lindsey's cheek, and her breathing hitched.

Lindsey patted his leg playfully. "Rusty's sounds

perfect." She shot up, suddenly full of energy. "I've gotta get ready. Give me thirty minutes."

He yelled after her skipping form, "I'll be back to pick you up."

Sissy turned to him when they heard Lindsey's footfalls on the stairs. "How's it going?"

"You've got eyes. Everything is great." He relaxed into the couch and marveled at the meaning in that answer. "I want to ask her to stay."

It felt like a weight had shifted in his life. One minute he was walking through life like a ghost in the fog, and the next he felt shocked back into life. Color was more vibrant and the air smelled sweeter. He even felt like he could breathe easier, as if he'd been gasping for air before, but now his lungs were clear.

"Finally." Sissy dragged out the word. "You better pull out all the good moves because I want my friend back too."

He sat up and rubbed his face vigorously. "What if I'm drawing dead?"

He wasn't as worried anymore about Lindsey's answer, but he still wasn't one hundred percent sure she would agree to stay. What would it do to him if she left again after the leaps and bounds they'd made together this week?

"If you ever want a full house, don't fold. You were dealt a bad hand six years ago, but this hand deserves its own chance. You gotta go all in on this one."

"How many poker references did you just make?" Dakota asked. He knew this was Sissy's way of softening the situation and distracting him from the potentially horrible outcome. He appreciated it, even if it was an immature tactic.

"You started it, but I think you're gonna like the river." She gave him a knowing wink.

"I'm kinda committed at this point. You just better not be bluffin'." He stood and made his way to the door. "I gotta go if I'm going to be back in thirty minutes."

"Just give it to her straight. Her tells are obvious, bro!" Sissy shouted at him as he approached the door.

He turned with his hand on the door to ask, "Was this your master plan to get us back together?"

She rolled her eyes. "Yes, Dakota. I decided to have a baby to lure your long lost love back home so you could woo her and fix your life. My work here is done."

"That's what I thought." He smiled and left to get ready for a night with his woman. He had plans to show her lots of reasons to stay.

CHAPTER 20
Lindsey

Sissy entered the bathroom just as Lindsey unplugged the hair dryer. She wondered what her friend thought about how cozy she and Dakota were today. There hadn't been lots of time to chat lately, and she was used to telling her best friend everything.

Sissy propped against the bathroom doorframe. "So," her friend paused for dramatic effect. "What's new?"

Lindsey turned to her with her head slightly tilted. "Well, Dakota showed me a beautiful piece of real estate yesterday. Would you happen to know anything about that?"

Sissy inspected her fingernails. "I may have heard of it... and helped design it. You're welcome."

"How did you keep that from me all this time? I tell you everything," Lindsey chided as she turned and glared at her friend's reflection in the mirror. Her neck grew hot when she thought about all the times Sissy had conveniently failed to mention the dream home Dakota had built in her absence.

Sissy pushed from the doorframe as she prepared to defend herself. "Except when it involves how you feel about Dakota. You've never talked about him even once since you left. It's been like a piece of our friendship—our lives—has been missing. You shut me out, and I wasn't about to bring it up if you were going to be less than interested in the information."

Sissy continued, shoving her finger at Lindsey. "It was a huge deal to him and his growth after you left, and it would have hurt me too if you had discarded it as nothing."

She made eye contact with her friend through the mirror. "I would have never thought it was nothing."

"How was I supposed to know that?" Sissy threw her hands up in mock surrender. "You certainly didn't act like anything involving Dakota was important to you."

"Could you at least have told me he almost died?" She wheeled around to face her friend in anger. She was losing her patience now that they had crossed into the forbidden topic of untrustworthiness.

"I was scared. I lost my best friend, and I couldn't lose my only brother too. Mom was a wreck, and she needed me. I told you I had laryngitis so we wouldn't have to talk for a while. I needed time to take care of my family. The ones you left behind," Sissy accused.

Never once had Sissy faulted her for leaving, and

Lindsey had been thankful. It had felt like she'd dodged a bullet all this time. Now her friend was finally confessing how she really felt, and it stung like she always knew it would. What hit home hardest was that Lindsey could understand everything Sissy felt. She deserved this, brought it on herself. How could she expect to never face the consequences of her actions if she came back here?

Lindsey's voice was obstructed by her tightening throat. "You never lost me, and I would have always been here for you *and* your family."

"How was I supposed to know that?" Sissy asked softly.

Lindsey embraced her friend in desperation. She let the feelings of love and warmth flow through her body and into her friend. She wished Sissy could feel her remorse. "I'm sorry. I'm so sorry I wasn't here for you."

Sissy hugged her tight. "You don't need to be sorry. I know you were doing what was best for you. I shouldn't have taken my problems out on you."

She pulled away from her friend and wiped a stray tear from Sissy's cheek. "I've been thinking about moving back."

Sissy didn't smile like she'd assumed. Actually, she looked concerned. "Are you sure that's the best idea?"

This was definitely not the reaction she expected from her friend. Her heart sank in fear. Had she missed something?

"Why wouldn't it be? I'd be closer to you and

Lydia. I could babysit, and we could hang out more. Of course, I would find an apartment or something. I wouldn't intrude here."

"That's not what I meant," Sissy said gravely. "What does this mean for you and Dakota? I don't want you to get his hopes up and let him down again. You need to be sure this is what you want."

"I want to be with him." She really did. She wanted the whole nine yards with him. She was sure of it now. "I don't want to run anymore. I want to come home. I *need* to come home for more than just Dakota." Her enemies were the clock and her own insecurities. They warred against her, throwing her two steps back to every one step forward.

Sissy hugged her again with misty eyes. Her friend had really turned into a sap since Lydia was born. "I just wanted to make sure you were ready. I know this week has been a lot to take in, but there are a lot of people who would love to have you back."

"What should I do? Dakota hasn't mentioned anything about it. Maybe he doesn't want me to move back." Lindsey rubbed her friend's back as her anxiety climbed. The thought of being rejected by Dakota after making this decision was unbearable.

"I'm pretty sure he does. I wouldn't worry about that. And don't get any stupid ideas about an apartment. You're welcome to live here as long as you want to stay. Tyler and Dakota can help you move in and we'll store any excess things you have until you're ready to move on. Just have fun tonight and don't wake me up when you come in." Sissy patted Lindsey's shoulder and turned to leave.

Lindsey resumed fixing her hair and thought of how incredibly lucky she was to have Sissy as a friend. Sissy may be all carefree and flighty, but the woman knew how to read people and handle any situation that came her way. She had a way of looking at all sides before making a decision, and Lindsey praised her for her insight. She felt a sense of peace knowing that she had a friend who would stand beside her no matter what and always do what was best for her.

She knew now that her goal over the next few days would be to mend every broken piece of her past to pave the way for the future she was determined to build.

CHAPTER 21
Lindsey

Dakota was the perfect gentleman as they started out for their date. He came to the door to pick her up wearing a solid black T-shirt and jeans. She'd always loved him in black, since the color harmonized with his dark hair and skin.

Sissy gave him a speech about taking care of Lindsey tonight, and he opened the hauntingly familiar Bronco door for her at Sissy's, and then again when they arrived at Rusty's.

Lindsey shouldn't have been surprised. He'd always done those things for her when they dated before. He did them without a conscious thought, and those million little things made up the great reasons why she loved him.

As they entered Rusty's, she stepped back in time. The place hadn't changed a bit. The wooden tables were arranged the same, the decor still hung steadfast to the walls as it had before, and even some of the restaurant staff were the same. The lights were turned down low, and a disco ball sat out of place above the rustic bar.

Dakota grabbed her hand and made his way to an open booth. She followed his heavy footfalls as she scanned her surroundings. Band equipment was set up on stage where Brian and Addie would play tonight.

"Dakota!"

A deep, male voice shouted from her left, and she looked to see their old friend Brian waving their way. Dakota gave a short wave in greeting, and she noticed there were other men sitting at the table with Brian.

"Let me just say hey, and we'll have the night to ourselves." He turned to lead her into the bench seat, but she turned to look back at Brian.

She realized she knew everyone at the table. They were her old friends, and the idea that she should become reacquainted if she intended to stay with Dakota and move back here entered her mind.

"No, let's sit with them. I'm sure they wouldn't mind," she said.

He gave her a look of skepticism. "Are you sure? This is supposed to be *our* date."

She gave him a light punch in the arm. "Come on. We can have some alone time when we leave here. Let's go hang out with your friends."

He took her hand as they snaked through the tables. "You know they're your friends too." It wasn't a question. It was a reminder.

She knew now why they kept her at a distance

upon her return. She'd caused Dakota a lot of trouble, and his friends had cared.

A chorus of greetings sounded as they approached the table. Brian kicked a chair away from the table beside him for her while Dakota took the seat between her and Declan. Addie sat on the other side of Declan, and she greeted Lindsey with a huge smile. She was glad to have already made at least one more girl friend.

"Little Lindsey." Brian's playful sweetness sparkled in his eyes as he propped his arm on the table to lean closer to her. His easy smile was radiant as always. He was a jokester, and she was sure he'd never grow up. He was a child at heart, and everyone needed a friend like Brian to diffuse the stress of life. "I heard you were back in town and putting the moves on our boy again."

"I think he put the moves on me, but I definitely couldn't resist his charms." She turned to Dakota and smiled as he wrapped an arm around the back of her chair.

Their old friend, Jake, made his way around the table, but it took her a second heartbeat to recognize him. Whoa, Jake had changed a lot.

He was strikingly handsome and sporting an extra twenty or so pounds of muscle. His brown hair was trimmed shorter than before, but the look suited him and made his usual sweet face seem harder than she remembered.

He wrapped her in a welcoming bear hug. "I can't believe you're back," Jake said with reverence.

She pulled back to look him up and down, taking in his beige uniform. "I'm sorry, are you a cop now?" she asked, and her voice hitched higher than usual.

"Cherokee County Deputy at your service." He tipped his imaginary hat with a smile.

"I should've guessed. It's so... perfect for you, Jake."

"Glad to have you back, Lindz." Jake slapped her on the back like he would with one of the guys and made his way back to his chair.

She settled back in her seat with a smile on her face and realized Ian sat across the table from her. She knew it was a little irrational, but she suddenly felt uncomfortable considering their last encounter at the barn a few days ago.

She soon found out that she shouldn't have worried. Ian was still surly, but his nasty attitude wasn't necessarily directed at her now. It didn't take long to remember that Ian was best kept at arm's length.

Ian hadn't always been coarse. He'd been wild and reckless once upon a time before his ex-wife, Julie, came along. She'd really done a number on him, and he couldn't seem to get over his "mad at the world" attitude.

They settled into a steady stream of banter as the night rolled on. Marcus strolled in about an hour later and made himself at home at their table.

This was just like the perfect dates she'd shared with Dakota so long ago, and any stress she felt in her life dissipated. There seemed to be a silent agreement against the mention of her impending departure tomorrow, and she was thankful.

Brian stood and stretched at about a quarter till eight. "I guess I'd better get ready." He chugged the last of his water and kissed Lindsey on the head before making his way to the stage.

Dakota snarled and stared daggers at Brian's back as Declan laughed and added, "You gotta shut him down quick or he'll be like a tick."

Lindsey and Addie laughed together, but the men at the table were suddenly eerily quiet.

Marcus, Ian, and Jake sat facing Lindsey, and each of them avoided eye contact with her. Ian didn't squirm for long before he stood and announced, "Incoming."

She watched as Ian made his way to the bar, and she turned toward Dakota in confusion.

A slightly familiar brunette woman bent over behind Dakota and wrapped her arms around his neck. Her silky black tank top fell open at her buxom breasts and an inch of her chemical tan midriff was showing above her belt. She obviously hadn't noticed Lindsey, and the whole situation shocked her into silence.

Dakota stiffened, but the woman wasted no time before she invaded his space. The girl's mauve lips brushed his ear, and Lindsey heard the whispered words that made her stomach roll.

"Hey, stranger." Her voice was low and seductive.

"I've been texting you all week. Why are you avoiding me?"

Her mind rejected the scene unfolding in front of her. There was no way this was happening. Did he know her? How often did he get propositioned so boldly?

Jealousy and humiliation swirled within her, and she knew her face must be the color of a ripe tomato. She felt hot, and it was difficult to breathe.

Dakota seemed to return to the present as he removed the woman's arms from his neck and turned to stand and face her. Lindsey suddenly felt blood rushing in her ears, and the sounds of the restaurant seemed to drift to her through water.

"I'm here with Lindsey tonight." He took Lindsey's sweaty hand and led her to her feet beside him. Her knees were unstable, and her heart beat fast.

"Actually, I'm with Lindsey every night," he amended as his arm wrapped around her waist and he pulled her to his side.

The woman jerked like she'd been electrocuted when she took a moment to look at Lindsey's face. "Lindsey!" Her eyebrows rose as she said the name like slander.

She suddenly knew that voice, and her heart sank to the floor. She was definitely going to be sick. "Oh, no. Tara?"

Tara Hanks. The stuck up mean girl that hadn't spared a second thought for anyone except her mighty clique in high school. The stereotypical popular cheerleader who had walked all over others to secure her social status.

Surely, this was a nightmare.

It wasn't a secret that Dakota and Lindsey spent all of high school and a few years after in a committed relationship, and Tara never even looked their way during that time. Dakota and Lindsey, along with their friends, with maybe the exception of Brian, were never popular enough to warrant her attention. Obviously, things had changed if she was familiar enough with Dakota to approach him the way she had.

Lindsey was still frozen in shock when Tara snarled, "Dakota, can we have a word outside?" It sounded like more of a demand than a request. She crossed her arms in disapproval.

"No, I'm on a date. If you need something just say it."

His voice wasn't condescending, but he was forceful enough to make his meaning clear. He wasn't leaving Lindsey's side, and she felt the sensation return slowly to her extremities that had grown numb during the encounter.

Tara threw her arms to her sides in a move reminiscent of a toddler's tantrum. "I need to talk to you in private." Her eyes never left his. It was like she was oblivious to the world around her. She had no concern for the patrons who were watching them as her volume rose.

"What could you possibly have to say? I've asked you to stop calling and texting me. I thought I was clear." Dakota threw the words at her, but his volume didn't rise as Tara's had.

At his comment, Tara stomped her foot in anger as she glared at him.

Jake inserted his broad shoulders in the small area between them. "Tara, I think you should go on about your business. If you've got something to say, say it and be gone. You've been pushing the line lately, and I don't want to have to get involved in a professional manner."

Jake was a master at taking control of situations. His innate authority was hard to ignore, and Tara wasn't completely immune, despite her strong will.

She held her stance, eyes locked on Dakota for a set of heartbeats before quickly turning on her three inch heels and stalking for the door.

Lindsey watched Tara's swaying hips as she walked and felt a stab in her heart. She wasn't normally a self-conscious person, but she couldn't help but look down at her plain white T-shirt, jeans, and sneakers without the twinkling of worry swimming in her head.

Lindsey was skinny, but she lacked the voluptuous body that Tara flaunted. Tara had the body of a tempting woman, and Lindsey felt like a child in comparison. Was Tara the type of woman Dakota was attracted to? She didn't dare breathe until the wooden door slammed shut behind Tara.

Dakota turned to her and grasped her shoulders before Tara was out of sight.

"Lindsey, I—"

"I think I'm gonna be sick." Actually, she was pretty certain she wanted to blow chunks right now. Humiliation, anger, and uncertainty swirled within her, and she turned to grab for her purse.

Dakota pulled out his wallet and handed some bills to Declan. "Cover me."

She was walking ahead of him to the door, but he caught up to her just as she reached the truck and opened the door for her. As it closed behind her, she felt it slamming shut on the innocence of their relationship. It was bound to happen at some point, but she wished it had never been brought to light.

He didn't start the truck, and he didn't look at her. His breathing was erratic, and his silence terrified her. They'd always been able to talk about anything and everything. If Dakota was hesitant to talk to her, she knew to prepare for the worst.

He finally spoke, and she found the nerve to turn to him in the dim light of the truck.

"I can't lose you again, Lindsey. Please let me explain." He rubbed his hands over his face and brought them to rest in a tight link at the base of his neck.

She'd never felt as broken as she did waiting for Dakota to speak. She wanted to hear something that would make her feel okay again.

"It's really nothing. At least, I hope it's nothing. I didn't want to say anything while we were still working things out."

Her eyes and nose tingled as she spoke. "I don't

know what that means." She knew he heard the shake in her voice.

"After I recovered from the wreck, I didn't want to be around anyone for a long time. My family was concerned, my friends were at a loss about how to bring me back to life, and I just stopped doing anything except going to work and building the house.

"It took over a year to get me back out of the house and hanging out with my friends again. When I started living again, Brian brought Tara to the barn where we were hanging out at one night and then set us up on a date. I didn't want to do it, but I knew I would have to do something or everyone I knew would keep hounding me. She was the first and only date I've been on since you left."

He stopped to look at her, and she could see the fear in his eyes. "I'm sorry."

She didn't speak, and he continued.

"After that, she wouldn't leave me alone. I told her I wasn't interested in going out with her again, but she wouldn't take no for an answer. I changed my number a few times, but she always finds it. Jake knows about it, but I haven't asked him to take any action because she hasn't actually done anything besides call and text."

The fire in Lindsey's chest was still hot, but dimming. "So you weren't ever in a relationship?"

"Never. I agreed to go on the date, and part of me hoped it would change things. I was tired of hurting." He rubbed his hands over his face in frustration. "And I was mad at you. I wanted you to be the one here wanting to date me, but you didn't want to talk to me or see me. I was angry. At the time, I think I gave in to punish you, even though I thought you would never know or care. I was also punishing myself. I didn't deserve you, and I knew I had to accept that. I knew I would hate myself for giving in, but in that moment when I had the least control over us," he gestured wildly between them, "I wanted to control something, and I chose wrong."

"Why was she angry? She made it sound like the two of you were seriously involved." The tears still came, but they rolled along quietly now.

He reached for her hand, and the contact was comforting. "I honestly have no idea why she acted like that. I don't answer her calls or texts, and I tell her the same thing every time she runs into me in public."

She looked away because she believed him, but she hated the situation anyway. "That was embarrassing."

"I'm sorry. I don't know what she was thinking blasting every word to the restaurant like that."

She still couldn't look at him, and he still hadn't started the truck. "That's not what I meant, but that was embarrassing too."

He slipped her hair behind her ear so he could turn her to face him. "What's going on in your head, Lindz?"

"She's..." she trailed off and had to swallow before she could finish the sentence. "She looks very different from me."

She could see his eyes narrow in the dim light shining from the bar. "I don't follow, Lindz."

"I look ordinary, and she—"

"Hold on just a minute," he interrupted and gripped her chin in resolve. "Is that something they told you in New York? You are anything but ordinary. You're the only woman I see."

She'd never encountered jealousy or the fear of cheating with Dakota, and it bruised her heart tonight. She trusted him with every fiber of her being.

He pulled her in and wrapped his arms around her like she might float away if he let go. She held onto him too and felt the humiliation and stress ease. She was wrapped in the arms of the man she loved, and the comfort she felt was enough to override the hurt.

"I'm sorry... about the way I acted tonight. It's not like I expected you to have never dated anyone. It was just a shock to come face to face with my worst nightmare tonight." She exhaled shakily, but at least she could breathe now.

"No, Lindz. I'm sorry. I hate everything about this, but it's over now. Please tell me this won't hurt us." He didn't let her go, and she didn't blame him. She wanted to keep holding on too.

"Nothing can hurt us, as long as we're in it together."

He pulled away and smiled. "I missed you, Lindz."

"I don't want you to miss me anymore," she whispered.

They didn't speak as he drove, and he didn't turn

off the truck before he turned to her in the drive in front of Sissy's house.

"I didn't get to dance with you tonight. We left before the music started." He picked up his phone and tapped for a moment before turning the radio up on Frank Sinatra's "One for my Baby."

He jumped from the truck and ran to open her door. Sinatra's croon filled the air as he opened her door and grabbed her waist to lift her from the seat and plant her feet on the ground as softly as a whisper on the wind.

"May I have this dance?"

"Of course." She smiled and rested her head on his chest as his hand slid around her waist.

They danced, and she realized the night was ending. She'd already planned to spend her last night with Sissy and Lydia. Dakota understood but swore he would be back first thing in the morning so they could go to church and spend some time together before she left. She wanted more time, more dances.

She wanted every dance to be Dakota's.

The future she'd once imagined for herself floated back to the surface and felt almost within reach.

CHAPTER 22
Dakota

Six Years Ago
New York City, New York

Dakota had imagined this night would play out a lot differently.

Not that he'd spent much time thinking about it since he'd flown in on a quick decision, but he hadn't expected to be sitting on the floor in the hall outside Lindsey's apartment for three hours. Oh, someone was surprised. It just happened to be him instead of Lindsey.

He looked at his watch. It was a quarter till two in the morning now, and she hadn't answered his last four calls—one when his plane touched down at JFK and one each hour since.

No, he'd assumed this night would play out

much differently. He hadn't seen Lindsey in four weeks—the longest stretch of time they'd been separated—and he couldn't take it anymore. He worked overtime, nights and weekends, to earn the money for this plane ticket. Being away from her was torture, but hopefully they wouldn't be apart for much longer.

He looked around in the empty hallway once more. Where was she? He could imagine a million terrible things that could have happened to her alone on the streets of New York City at night.

The breath he'd been inhaling stopped short. What if she wasn't alone?

What if she was with someone else?

He stood and started to pace. It was all part of the routine. Pace, sit, pace, sit. Worry, panic, worry, panic.

He was about to sit after fifteen laps up and down the hallway when he heard footsteps on the stairs.

Lindsey opened the stairway door and entered the hallway doubled over, eyes closed mid-laugh. Two women followed behind her in the throes of the same bubbling laughter. She was wearing makeup, and her short, blonde hair was pulled half-back by hidden clips or something. He could count the number of times he'd seen her wear makeup on two hands, and he'd never seen her hair any way other than straight or in a ponytail.

They stumbled a few steps into the hall before Lindsey noticed him and halted. The other women instantly stopped, and one reached into her bag, presumably for a weapon, but Lindsey laid a hand on her arm and said, "It's all right, Jean. I know him."

She knew him? That's all? She obviously didn't want her friends to know she had a boyfriend.

Apparently, she hadn't mentioned him.

Shame was clear on her face as she turned to her friends and said, "Sorry, guys. I'll call you tomorrow."

"You're not going to introduce me, Lindz?" He crossed his arms over his chest to prevent fidgeting. The adrenaline coursing through his body was enough to light a fire. He didn't care if she went out with her friends, as long as she was safe about it, but to deny him in front of others was something that she'd never done before.

Sheepishly, she turned to the women. "This is Dakota. Dakota, this is—"

"No way, Lindz. That's all I get? I'm just Dakota to you now? You sure there isn't more? I don't know, maybe eight years more?" He was angry now, and he couldn't care less. He was seething on the inside.

Ignoring her friends now, she unlocked the door to her apartment and said, "Let's go inside and talk."

He felt it then. That tiny snap at the end of their relationship. Talking was what he came for, but it hadn't been the talk he felt waiting for him on the other side of that door.

His anger and fear mingled into a panic he tried to hide. What was happening right now? From where he stood, he couldn't piece together how he'd gotten here.

She stood holding the door open, waiting for him

to enter. When he finally moved, the footfalls of his heavy boots echoed down the hallway. The sound was completely out of place in this New York apartment building, and he latched onto the anomaly just to distract his frantic mind.

He'd been inside her new apartment a handful of times since she moved in a few months ago, and he still felt as claustrophobic as the first time. It wasn't that the space was small. It was the windows. You could see outside, but only as far as the neighboring building across the alley.

"I'm sorry, Dakota. I didn't know you were coming, and we all got good news about jobs today and decided to celebrate." She roamed around the small apartment, paying attention to anything but him as she spoke.

"That's not why I'm mad, Lindz. First, I was worried about you because you haven't answered my calls."

"It was loud where we were. I didn't realize..."

"I'm not looking for excuses. I'm glad you're all right, and I'm past that. What I'm not past is the fact that you looked like a deer caught in the headlights when you saw me, and you didn't want to introduce me to your friends. What's wrong, Lindz? I just assumed you'd be happy to see me. It's been a month."

She finally looked at him and sank onto the sofa. "I'm sorry. I feel like I have a double life. My life here is one thing, and my life with you is another." She studied her fingernails as she continued. "I feel like I'm betraying you when I'm happy here."

"As long as you're not cheating on me, then there's no reason to feel that way. You can be as happy as you want here, and I won't stop that. I'm working on getting us together, but it's a slow process. Just trust me. I'm going to fix this."

"And see, that's where we differ. I don't see anything wrong." She was defensive now, and he couldn't understand why.

"What's wrong is we're apart. I want us together." He'd never had a way with words, but somehow Lindsey had always understood what he meant. Something inside him screamed that she wouldn't this time.

"You can't move here, Dakota."

"Watch me. I'm coming, and we won't have anything to worry about."

He crossed the room and knelt before her on the floor. Her hands were shaking, and he took them in his to steady them. "Don't worry. I have a plan." He was staring into her eyes hoping she could read his soul.

"You can't move here." Her voice shook, and he couldn't process the words together.

"I'm moving. I just need time. I have some things to take care of, and I'll be here before you know it."

She stood and her hands were pulled from his grasp. He felt the loss instantly, but he wouldn't understand until later that the pain had been a shockwave signaling their last touch.

She hugged her arms around her middle as she

paced the living area. "I think you should go. We both know this won't work anymore. We're too different now. You think I don't see how unhappy you are here when you visit?"

Words swam around him in a muffled haze, but he couldn't hear them. She continued to talk as he stood there stunned. He caught bits and pieces of her breakup speech, and when he couldn't take it anymore, he walked out the door and down the hall.

This. Was. Not. Happening.

The sound of her elevated words that would haunt him in the coming years shut off as the stairway door closed behind him.

He didn't even say good-bye.

Present Day
Carson, Georgia

Dakota woke with the echoing thud of a closing door in the recesses of his dream. Cold sweat covered his face and neck at the memory of that door closing on his past and future. The warmth that lingered in the first half of October was gone, and he felt chilled and alone in the bedroom.

That metallic thud had caught him off guard a number of times over the years. That unexpected omen of loss was a burden waiting in the shadows of his dreams, and he wondered why it came to him today of all days.

Then he remembered that today was close enough in character to that long ago day in New York City to leave him uneasy. She was leaving again, and this time he intended to do a better job of stopping her. He planned to change her mind this time. They were older and wiser now, and he was sure they both understood everything at stake the second time around.

She told him she made a mistake. She said she was sorry. They mended fences, and he didn't feel the fear he had the last time.

He sat up in bed and rubbed his hands over the stubble of his jaw before reaching for the drawer of the bedside table.

A black ring box sat nestled amongst a litter of pens and scraps of home designs and drawings that came to him in the moments before sleep. He picked it up gently, thinking it seemed smaller than he remembered.

The ring hadn't been removed from this drawer since he first put it there when he moved into the house. He hadn't felt the urge to look at it, but he wanted it close enough that he wouldn't forget it.

He studied the box carefully for a moment before opening it. The box was lighter than he expected, and it seemed like such a tiny token to have such a larger-than-life significance.

When he opened the box for the first time since he purchased the ring, he was relieved to realize he hadn't forgotten exactly what the ring looked like in all these years. There had been times when he wondered if the image in his head still matched the real ring, but even his curiosity couldn't have brought him to open that box again. Opening Pandora's Box before now had seemed like a death wish.

The white gold set was still nestled into the black velvet pillow but slightly skewed. The thin band of diamonds was curved to perfectly hug the perimeter of the single oval diamond surrounded by smaller diamonds.

When he saw this ring, he knew it would be perfect for her. She was well rounded, and the halo of diamonds reminded him of a crown. He recalled thinking that she was his queen, and she deserved this crown.

He aligned the engagement ring and band and closed the box. He'd been twenty-two when he bought the set, and he'd worked long, hard hours to afford it. Now, he was financially stable, and he still felt a surge of pride for the ring he held. He wouldn't trade this ring for all the money in the world. He'd meant to give it to her once, and it was still meant for her. This time he would make sure it landed on her finger.

He sprang from the bed with a purpose. He was showered, shaved, and dressed for church before eight in the morning. Waiting another minute to see her wasn't an option. The flood gates were open, and he couldn't hold off the things he needed to say.

The Bronco hummed as he sped to Tyler and Sissy's house. He knew Lindsey hadn't left yet because she promised to stay for church with him, but his foot sat heavier on the accelerator without his permission.

He and Lindsey were on the same page this time. They wanted the same things, and that made all the difference. She'd gone, flourished, found herself, and now she was back. He'd lived a half-life, but he wouldn't trade the souvenirs if it meant he could have her now.

He pulled the Bronco into the semi-circle drive in front of her Maxima and leapt from the vehicle before it came to a complete stop. Three long strides found him at the front door, and he didn't bother knocking. He was a storm breaking without warning.

She was in the living room passing Lydia to Sissy when he saw her and came to a halt.

He ran to this point, and now he found himself stopped short. She always caught him off guard. He'd known Lindsey for as long as he could remember, and every new meeting felt like a punch in the gut. She was perfection, a beacon of light, a gravitational force he couldn't shake.

Her brown hair fell around her shoulders like a waterfall, and her brown eyes were hazy with unshed tears as she turned to him. The autumn weather had finally made an appearance, and she wore a long-sleeve Carson High School shirt with a growling wildcat on it he recognized.

Starstruck, he didn't speak right away. He just took her in and basked in the light of the woman he loved.

He ached to go to her, but there was something he needed to get off his chest first.

He took the first step slowly. After all, nothing was going to happen if he didn't get the first one out of the way.

"I can't compete with the boy I used to be." Another tentative step.

"I didn't know what losing you felt like then. I didn't know what dying was." His gaze didn't falter from hers. "I hadn't hit rock bottom yet."

He was getting closer, and he could see a shimmering tear on her cheek now. "I didn't know what it was to be lonely, and I hadn't lived with years of regret because I didn't fight harder for us."

Her eyes were red, and she wore a look of pain. "Dakota—"

He cut her off. He had to get this out now. "I didn't beg you to stay, but I wanted to so bad." Only five feet separated them, and he had to restrain himself from closing the gap. He wanted to mold her into himself until they were one.

Then he stopped his forward progress. "The man I am now knows I can't afford to lose you. It's wrong and selfish of me to ask you to settle for the shell of a man I've become, but I'm doing it anyway.

"Lindsey, please come home. We've only had a week, but I don't want to be away from you."

She was crying in earnest now, and for the first time, he was terrified of her response. He wished she'd say something.

Sissy was crying, and she blurted, "I already told her she could live with us."

He lifted Lindsey's chin to make her look at him. "Will you stay, Lindz?"

Her arms came around his neck quickly and she squeezed tight. "I'm sorry. I'm sorry I did this to us. I'm sorry I left," the words rushed from her mouth.

"That's not what this is about, Lindz. Are you staying?" He prayed. He asked God for help. Prayed she would find favor with him and want to stay. He needed an answer now.

"Yes. I'm sorry. I'm sorry I pushed you away. I'm sorry I broke us for so long. I want everything with you again."

She shook with her sobs, and he clung to her as soon as he heard her affirmation.

"I love you, Lindsey." He rubbed her head and buried his face in her hair, breathing in the scent of her as if he'd been drowning. The air around them entered his nose like a wave of pleasure heightening his euphoria.

"I love you, too. I love you, too." She sounded almost frantic as if she'd been holding her breath, unsure if the life-giving air would return in time. "I'm sorry—"

"Don't say that again. We're past all that, and it's over. This is us again."

"I have to go back though." The sadness in her voice kicked him in the heart too.

"I know."

"Just to put in my notice at work and handle my apartment. I'll get started right away." Her words were growing stronger with her resolve.

"I'll be there next weekend to help you pack and bring the first load home." They were filling in pieces of the plan together.

"Home." She said the word in confusion.

"Yeah, home."

He kissed her then. He couldn't have stopped himself for anything on earth. Lindsey was back in his arms, and everything felt right again. Her lips were soft against his, and nothing else mattered.

He heard a soft whimper behind him, and Lindsey pulled away. They both looked to the sound to find Sissy hugging Lydia to her chest with tears on her face.

"Sorry I'm such a sap. It's the—"

"Hormones. We know." Lindsey was understanding as she wrapped her friend in a hug, careful not to bother the baby.

"I'm just so glad you're getting smart. I've missed you."

He sank onto the sofa and buried his head in his hands in relief as Lindsey and Sissy celebrated. Tyler came to sit beside him and clapped him on the back.

"Congrats, man. You got her back."

"Yeah. It still feels like a dream." He looked up to find her radiant smile and prayed he could always keep her this happy.

He sighed. "I feel like the first hurdle is over, but now I have to get through the next few weeks."

"Ah, that'll be a piece of cake. You got this." Tyler sounded so sure, but Dakota was terrified.

"I just need her home."

He stood as she approached, but she stopped short and hesitated. He felt lucky, invincible, honored with her beside him.

She pushed onto her toes and linked her fingers at the base of his neck before he wrapped his arms around her waist and lowered his forehead to hers.

After all this time, they still wouldn't say good-bye.

They would never say good-bye.

CHAPTER 23

Lindsey

Dakota grabbed her hand as they stepped into the sanctuary of the church. The small gesture sent waves of support to her troubled heart. While she was more than happy, elated even, to be moving back to Carson and beginning a new chapter of her life with Dakota and her friends, she was bone tired.

The happiness she felt about the changes in her life were battling with her will to change. The uneasiness she felt was due to the one part of her life she still hadn't set to rights—her soul.

The church looked much the same, but she could spot a few updates since her last visit. The sound system was much larger and more high-tech, and she thought the pew cushions had once been a deep maroon instead of the Union blue they were now.

Despite the changes she could observe, the building itself *felt* much the same to her as she entered.

The memories of peace and happiness stood side-by-side with her newfound anxiety.

She shouldn't have been surprised that most of the church members were the same as six years ago. The music director and preacher of her childhood still hung around the podium finishing up their meeting about the upcoming service.

Dakota stayed by her side as they made happy greetings and revealed the news of her homecoming to old friends she hadn't spoken to since her departure. Everyone shared her excitement to return to Carson, so she couldn't understand why her chest felt like a weight was pressing into her.

They took their seats with Sissy on her left and Barbara to Dakota's right. The long pew was filled with their family. Yes, these people were her family too. They were more than friends, and she'd spent her life with them.

The thought hit her that one day the people who sat beside her in this sanctuary really *would* be her family. She and Dakota had always assumed they would be married eventually. Even when they were apart, she hadn't entertained the idea that she would marry anyone else. The thought felt wrong.

The turmoil that began as kindling a few hours ago was building to a substantial roar within her as the music director took his place at the podium and the congregation quieted. She sucked in a deep breath and released it slowly just as Sissy grasped her hand.

Lindsey forced her mouth to form a reassuring

smile but didn't look at her friend. Sissy knew she was struggling this morning, but the gesture would let her know she was trying.

"Good morning." The music director's charismatic voice filled the cavernous room.

Russell Gibson was a sweet, rotund man who was probably in his early sixties now. His snow-white beard was neatly brushed down and covered his full cheeks, upper lip, and down over his jaw. Wisps of the same ghostly hair were combed over the top of his balding head and in a full horseshoe around the rest.

Mr. Gibson had taken her under his wing when she was in middle school. She joined a small theater group in town about that time, and while acting was her goal, she realized singing would have to grace her resume of talents as well in order to be seriously considered for roles one day.

Her voice lessons lasted until she moved to New York, and they'd been invaluable. He taught her everything she knew. From reading music to playing the piano, he'd been her mentor.

Mr. Gibson announced the page number of the first hymn of the worship service then made eye contact with her. She smiled at his choice of song just as the lyrics sank in her core. She didn't believe in coincidences. The hymn for the day was chosen long before this morning, but God certainly wanted her to listen carefully to the words of "Softly and Tenderly."

She stood and sang along with the congregation as the words of God pleading with weary, lost souls to find their home with Him. *Why this song, Lord? I've already chosen to move back home.*

Even as she questioned God's message for her, she knew the answer. He wasn't calling her home to any place. She was being beckoned home to her Father. Her struggles this past week about her relationship with God were building to a crescendo, and the beat of her heart raced with anticipation.

She wasn't being called home to Georgia or Dakota. She was being called home to Him. Home wasn't a place; it was her Heavenly Father. She may have lost her way for a while, but this was the true way home.

The path He'd chosen for her became clearer in her mind as she listened to the worship service and then the message brought by the preacher. The words were strangling her, sitting on her shoulder, begging for understanding and attention.

By the time Mr. Gibson ascended the altar again, her heart was near to bursting and her throat stung with the conviction she felt. She fought against the urge to move. She battled with invisible hands that felt close enough to real, pushing her toward that altar.

The invitation began to play, a song so familiar that every word and note settled within her before it was played. Dakota's words from a few nights before danced in her head, but one was louder than the others. *Repent.*

She lifted her head, eyes filling with tears, and turned to Sissy. Her friend moved to make room for

Lindsey to pass and Tyler did the same, but she felt Dakota grab her hand and move to follow her. She looked into those blue eyes and shook her head. She knew he would follow her to the ends of the earth, but this was something she needed to do on her own.

The first and only time she'd gone to the altar, Dakota followed her. She'd been a meek twelve-year-old girl terrified of her upcoming teen years and entering a life that seemed too vast for her understanding. Before that moment, she'd only been Sissy's friend. After, she'd been irrevocably tied to Dakota for life.

The last time, he'd held her hand as they walked down the aisle of the church and knelt. He held her as she opened her heart to God. He prayed over her as her heart filled with the Holy Spirit. Ever since that day, Dakota had proven to her that he would be her rock, and that was the moment both of their lives changed.

She dedicated her life to Christ, and Dakota and God both chose to stand by her for the rest of their days. Dakota had been fourteen and struggling to know when he could call himself a man and fighting the worries of teenage years, like how his friends and the people around him would perceive everything he did.

In that pivotal moment, he chose to take a young girl under his wing and protect her. This time, all these years later, she knew how he felt about her. She didn't question his dedication or love for her, just as she didn't question God. The one who needed to reassure others of her relationships was Lindsey.

This time, she needed to go to God alone. She'd lost her way, failed God. Now, she needed to make things right. Her memories were made up of this loving, selfless man standing beside her, but she couldn't live in the past anymore. She couldn't wait to make a life with him filled with better days, but she needed to fix herself first.

She let her fingers slip from his hand as her body moved of its own accord. When she stepped into the aisle, she eyed the altar and prayed. *Please meet me there, Lord. I want to come to you.*

When she reached the front of the enormous room filled with watching eyes, she knew she needed to get down on her knees before she could truly stand again.

Lindsey often thought of her life like a play made up of a series of acts. She could feel the curtain closing on a scene, but a new act was coming. This would be her time to shine. The close of a fickle world that fell to pieces meant the madness before rebirth, the darkness before dawn.

Her knees touched the ground, and she prayed. She prayed for forgiveness, she begged for guidance, and she repented. She threw her soul into the words, then rested back on her heels.

She looked up to find Jim Pearson, the preacher, standing before her with an outstretched hand and a smile on his face. Taking his warm hand in hers, she stood to meet his smiling face. "Welcome home, Lindsey."

The tears burst from her in an instant. Sobs shook her body, and she fell into his waiting arms. It was happiness. Pure, uninhibited joy sprang from her, and she released the flood of emotion the only way she knew how.

When she recovered enough to release the preacher, she moved to return to her seat with a smile that stretched her cheeks. She didn't deserve this happiness, but she'd been gifted the soul-saver anyway. God had a powerful way of pulling you into His arms.

Dakota met her at the end of the pew and pulled her to him. She heard the sniffles peppering through the small church and opened her eyes to see her family and friends watching her with quivering lips and tear-stained cheeks.

This was home, and she was right where she belonged.

CHAPTER 24
Lindsey

Lindsey closed the trunk of her Maxima as her mother descended the last step of the apartment building. "Anything left?" Lindsey yelled.

"Nothing. Clean as a whistle," her mom responded.

Lindsey's phone rang, and she fished it from the back pocket of her jeans as she and her mother opened the car doors. It was Dakota, and a spark came to life inside her. She missed him terribly, and her heart raced knowing she was on her way to see him now.

"Hey. We're getting in the car now," she answered in a giddy voice she hardly recognized as her own.

"Thank goodness. What's your ETA?" Dakota sounded relieved.

She looked to her mother who was programming the GPS for Carson. "It looks like... around four o'clock."

"Perfect. You think you'd be up for a surprise tomorrow night?" She could hear his excitement, and as tired as she was, her heart beat even faster in anticipation.

"What did you have in mind?" She was smiling, but it couldn't be helped. She always thought it was a little silly to smile while talking on the phone. The person you were talking to couldn't see your facial expressions.

"It's a surprise, Lindz. As in, I'm not telling."

"Um, you know Mom is with me," she reminded him.

"I remembered. She can come too. This is a 'the more the merrier' kind of date."

Sure, she enjoyed romantic dates with Dakota, but they usually had just as much fun hanging out in a group.

"Great. Hold on a sec." Lindsey moved the phone from her face as she asked her mom, "Want to come out with me and Kota tomorrow night? I have no idea where we're going, but he said you're welcome to come."

"I'd love to, but I need some time to rest, baby."

She was extremely grateful her mom had flown in to help her move, and she definitely understood the exhaustion. "You sure?" Lindsey asked.

"I'm positive. Y'all have fun, and let me sleep. I have plans to spend some time with Barbara before I fly out anyway."

Her mom had always been friendly with Dakota's

mom, and she knew they hadn't seen each other since her parents' divorce and her mother's subsequent move out of state. She was happy the two planned to catch up.

Kathy and Barbara had been inseparable since Dakota's dad died. Her mother took to Barbara's side without a word and had been an unfaltering friend ever since. Barbara encouraged Kathy to find ways to become her own person after the divorce, which led to her move to North Carolina in search of a new place to thrive. The two women may not have been physically close, but Lindsey knew they hadn't drifted apart, just as she and Sissy kept up their friendship. It didn't matter that they lived on opposite sides of the country.

She was thankful for her mother's help these last few days, but she was even happier to just be with her. She missed her mom since she moved to California with Dan, her step-father.

She liked Dan as much as any other person. Dan was friendly, but just pretentious enough to make it noticeable. He was Dan. Not Danny. Not Daniel. His name was Dan, and for some reason he called her mother Katherine. Sure, Katherine was her mother's real name, but everyone called her Kathy.

She wasn't sure if the name came from the wealthier class he waltzed in now or the fact that her mother may very well have introduced herself as Katherine to him when they met in order to make herself sound more sophisticated.

Marrying into a higher tax bracket hadn't changed

her mother all that much. Lindsey kept her mother informed of the developments with Dakota, and Kathy jumped on a plane to help with the move without a second thought when she told her about it. Whatever the reasons that brought her together with her mother, she was always glad to be with her.

Barbara graciously offered to let her mother stay in her guest room while she was helping Lindsey move her belongings to Carson. Truly, her families merged well.

Lindsey returned to the call with Dakota. "Mom said she'll sit this one out, but I'm game."

"Good. See you in a few. Love you."

"Love you too."

She hung up the phone and followed the initial instructions provided by the talking GPS.

The last two weeks passed in a blur. Two weeks was long enough, and she worked long hours to make sure she could get home as fast as possible.

The law firm she worked for didn't give her a hard time, but they'd asked that she work the full two-week notice out to make sure she could train her replacement. She agreed, since she wouldn't consider leaving them high and dry. The training hadn't been as extensive as she anticipated, since her organizational skills made things easy to find and figure out for her replacement.

The day after she left Carson, Ian called and asked her if she would be interested in taking up the books at the hardware store he and Brian owned. He told her

Dakota mentioned to him she was looking for a job, and he and Brian agreed that a bookkeeper would ease a lot of his stress. Ian didn't delegate well, but he trusted Lindsey and wanted to snatch her up before someone else made a move.

Ian's job offer was a blessing. She was so close to pulling completely out of debt, and the move hadn't set her back as much as she expected. She wouldn't have a gap between jobs now, and she'd be right back on track to cleaning out that debt from New York.

She'd always been good at numbers, but that also translated into a knack for finances. Her budgeting over the last few years saved her, and a little investing sweetened the pot.

She refused to bring her baggage into her new relationship with Dakota. When they finally did decide to get married, she didn't want to put strain on the relationship. Dakota worked himself ragged for years now and had something to show for all his hard work. She'd played in the big city and gotten into a bind that wasn't his fault. She felt liberated knowing the past was fading behind her as she worked herself out of debt and as she drove south.

With that one uncertainty off her shoulders, she felt her motivation kick into an even higher gear. Every evening she packed and made phone calls about the apartment. She quickly worked out a deal to be let out of her lease, and she didn't even care that she would have to pay a fee to do it.

Dakota drove up to Holly Springs last weekend

with an enclosed trailer and carted all of the boxes she'd packed so far back to Carson. He told her he wanted to help her unpack, so they spent late nights on video calls where he ran around her new room at Sissy's house indicating possible homes for her things while she laid in bed laughing at him. She was breaking down an old apartment and building a new home at the same time.

Dakota was a life-changer for her. The elusive home she'd searched for was now found in the eyes and arms of the man who hadn't given up on her. The man who forgave her for any pain she'd caused him was welcoming her home with open arms.

Going home felt right. It felt like a step forward. It felt like finding the right answer after searching for... well, years. It felt like a second chance at life, love, and happiness.

This time, she'd fight for the people who'd been there for her when she hadn't done the same for them. Loyalty screamed in her veins, and fire licked in her blood.

It was time to go home.

Dakota

Dakota hung up the call with Lindsey and returned the phone to his back pocket before turning back to the construction site. They were working on a garage addition for the probate judge in town, and the cool air of late October wasn't enough to stave off the heat of exertion.

Declan was still bent over the boards that lay parallel to the ground over a set of sawhorses. He was thankful every day that Declan was willing to go into the construction business with him when he was discharged from the Army.

As far as Dakota could tell, Declan's combat injuries didn't hinder his work on site. Dakota watched his friend with a careful eye for months trying to detect any weakness, but he ultimately found none. Dec showed up for work without fail and never complained, and an extra pep had entered his step since Addie came into his life.

"What's the word?" Declan asked, looking up from the boards.

"She's on her way. Should be here this afternoon." Dakota grabbed his nail gun and went back to work.

"This is it, man. She's really coming home for good?" He could hear a slight relief in his friend's voice now.

"I hope so. I think it's a little late to turn back now, since half her stuff is already unpacked at Sissy's house." He really didn't want to hash out his worst fear right now.

"Addie sure is happy about it. She likes Lindsey, and she needs more friends. She hasn't had that in a long time."

Declan's girlfriend, Adeline, was kept under lock and key by her ex-boyfriend for years. Addie was just now beginning to find out what living her own life really meant, and Dakota still clenched his jaw sometimes when he thought of the purple bruises on her face the first time he met her.

He knew Declan wanted Addie to have all the things she'd been denied during those years stuck in an apartment at her ex's will. Dakota wanted the same things for Lindsey, and that's why he couldn't fault her for going to New York. She'd wanted to do something for herself, and she deserved to go after it. Fate just happened to bring her back to him now with a clearer view on life.

Declan didn't chat much on the job site, or at all for that matter, but today, it was nice to hear his friend encouraging him that things would work out for the best with Lindsey.

Declan wiped the sweat off his brow as he continued. "I sure am glad the two of you worked things out now because I know she would never intentionally hurt you. Addie needs a friend, and I know firsthand that Lindz is a good one."

Declan was right about that. Lindsey didn't have a clue what Declan and Addie were going through when she rode into town a few weeks ago, but she'd helped in her own way. She'd also weathered her own insecurities about leaving during those years. No one could deny that she was a good friend. She'd been patient with Declan during high school when he didn't care to talk —about anything. He wouldn't be the expressive friend he knew now without Lindsey's help.

Dakota kept to his work and didn't give his full attention to his friend. "You were right... at the hospital."

"'Bout what?" Declan asked as he lined up the boards.

"I know why you're trying to work things out with your dad. It makes sense, and I get your end game." He stopped to look up at his friend now. He would find it hard to forgive his friend's deadbeat dad, but Declan had his eyes on the prize—a family with kids who could know their only grandparent.

"When you know, you know, and there isn't much point in waiting." He knew Declan would propose to Addie one day, but he knew his friend was waiting to make sure she had time to live her own life first. For now, his friend was preparing for the future he wanted for Addie and himself.

Dakota could respect his friend for getting his ducks in a row. He'd spent years doing the same thing before and after Lindsey left. Now, Lindsey was on her way home, and he could provide a life she deserved.

Declan cracked one of his infrequent grins. "Glad you see it my way."

CHAPTER 25
Lindsey

The next day, Lindsey and her mother planned to meet Addie, Barbara, and Sissy for lunch at Sandy's, the chic restaurant inside Bernard's Hotel. Dakota told her he would be going to work before daylight so that he could come home early for their surprise date. She was eager to spend some time with her mother and friends before her mom left for her home on the west coast.

Walking down main street beside her mother felt surreal. They enjoyed a close bond. They used to take day trips to flea markets, fall festivals, the beach, you name it. Her mother was a constant in her life, and she wouldn't trade it for the world. Her father was absent more than not, and her mother hadn't begrudged the solitude of childrearing, though Lindsey knew it would've been easy for any person to give in to.

Barbara and Sissy were always invited to any mother-daughter function they cooked up, and for a while after Sissy's dad died, the trips had been only Lindsey, Kathy, and Sissy when Barbara had needed time to herself.

Now that Lindsey had spent time with Sissy and her new daughter, Lydia, she respected her own mother on an even higher level. Lydia consumed the lives of everyone around her and left them ragged at times.

Her own mother had done all of that alone. She was certain her dad hadn't taken time off work when she'd been born, and she was sure her dad had thought parenting was a woman's job. She'd never been close with her dad, but he hadn't made any effort to get to know her.

"Mom, you know I love you, right?" She couldn't keep it in right now. The words had to be said again.

"Well, of course. You tell me every day. I love you too, sweetie." Her mother's heels clicked on the sidewalk in a steady rhythm as she extended her hand and took Lindsey's into her own.

Though her mother was sleek and feminine, Kathy never minded that her daughter was a mix of girlish features with tomboy tendencies. Lindsey liked to look good, but she also itched to get dirty sometimes.

Today, she wore white-washed jeans, Chucks, and a royal-blue long-sleeve shirt featuring the name and logo of the local Mexican restaurant in town. She'd owned the shirt since high school, and it was her go-to for comfort. In contrast, her mother wore a sheer beige blouse that cinched at her waist and form-fitting, white skinny slacks.

She followed her mother into Sandy's. "Wow, this place has come a long way."

Sandy's was an average restaurant when she left Carson six years ago. Now, the place looked like it would fit right in with some of the chic boutique restaurants in many larger cities. Not New York, of course, but Raleigh or Durham for sure.

"Oh, yes. Barbara told me all about it when they renovated a couple of years ago. She raves about this place." Her mother waltzed through the restaurant to the hostess podium as if she were the guest of honor.

The walls were a soft blush color accented with pastel mint. Ivory and mauve tea cups adorned shelves on the walls and succulents were scattered in pots along a half wall that divided the restaurant.

"Is the food as good as the atmosphere?" Lindsey asked. The soft scent of green tea wafted in the air as the hostess led them past a bar.

No wonder Barbara insisted on making reservations. The place was crowded, even for lunch hour. The hostess led them to a booth nestled in the far corner of the restaurant just as Addie came walking up behind them.

"Hey, guys."

Lindsey reached for Addie and wrapped her arms around her neck. "Hey, Addie, this is my mom, Kathy."

The ladies shook hands and made their greetings before sitting and opening the menus.

"How was your drive yesterday?" Addie asked as she browsed the lunch specials.

"It was long, but we had lots to talk about, so it wasn't too bad."

Barbara approached their table a few minutes later but didn't sit down. "Kathy, I just saw Angie Matthews on my way in, and when I told her I was meeting you here, she was thrilled to hear you're in town. Come on, she wants to chat a bit."

Barbara said her hellos to Lindsey and Addie as Kathy stood to accompany her back to Ms. Matthews' table, and then the two were left alone.

"It's so good to see them back together. They've been friends for so long," Lindsey remarked.

Addie stared after them as they walked away. "That's so sweet. It's so great to have friends like that."

"Speaking of, I'm so glad we met. It's been great talking with you these last few weeks. Dakota has been amazing helping me with the move, but sometimes you just need girl talk."

"Believe me, I don't take girl talk for granted. I'm just now getting used to having friends at all, and it's..." Addie looked out the window at the bustling downtown street. "I'm so lucky to have you and Sissy."

Lindsey sometimes forgot about Addie's troubled past. Her friend was so charismatic and happy these days, imagining her locked up and alone still hurt her heart. "I know, Addie. I'm thankful to know you too."

Lindsey looked up, and her happiness fell as she spotted a familiar face across the room. Tara Hanks was stepping out of a booth with another dark-haired woman. She was dressed in a navy-blue, form-fitting wrap dress with nude pumps. Her dark hair fell in shiny waves over a porcelain colored scarf around her neck.

Suddenly, Lindsey's faded jeans and Converses felt itchy. She fidgeted just as Addie caught sight of Tara.

"She always looks so unhappy," Addie whispered.

For the first time, Lindsey looked at Tara in a different light. Sure, she was beautiful, but Addie was right. Her features were sharper than glass, and her mouth never turned up at the corners. The scowl on her face marred what would've been a beautiful profile. Her eyes were full of feline malice, but they held the promise of venom like a snake.

Tara always looked as if she were ready to strike.

Lindsey tried not to watch her as she glided toward the door, but Tara spotted her just as she was passing their table. In that small moment, the indifference on her face turned to outright hatred.

As they passed out of Tara's line of sight, the woman slowly turned her attention from them and held her chin higher than was natural.

She felt Addie squeeze her hand to get her attention. "Hey, don't worry about her."

Addie sounded so sure, but Lindsey's heart pounded at the memory of that night at Rusty's when Tara entered her life with a bang. Addie was there for the whole show that night, so she knew the reasons for Lindsey's tension.

The hustle and bustle of the restaurant around her seemed to fade into the sound of breaking waves in time with her pulse. Her body felt as if it were filled with lead, and she sank farther into the cushion of the booth.

"I'm sorry. It's hard not to be affected by her. She's... intimidating." How did one person have the power to ruin her fun afternoon with her friends?

"Why? She's stern and seems a bit cruel at times, but her words aren't sticks and stones. They can't hurt you. At least, that's what I've told myself before."

Lindsey gnawed her bottom lip. "Should I be worried about her?"

She didn't want to be concerned about Tara. The flip side of that coin meant that worrying over Tara meant a lack of trust in Dakota, but she trusted him completely. He didn't deserve to be second guessed.

"No." Addie was so certain in her response. "I've seen her approach Dakota the same way she did at Rusty's a few weeks ago. He held the same stance then as he did when you saw them together. I'm not just saying this to make you feel better. I see him with you, and the difference is like night and day. I don't know Tara, but I know she's only out for number one. I've seen her interact with people before. She's not friendly, and she's not a threat to your relationship. She uses people, and I think that's what she's trying to do with Dakota. I can't think of another explanation for it."

Lindsey took a deep breath through her nose. She knew her friend was right, and she needed to move forward without letting the past interfere with the future she was building now. "I know. I trust him."

Addie had a past that could easily cripple her future if she let it, but the strong woman sitting beside her refused to bow to the unsavory circumstances life dealt her. Looking only at the surface of their new relationship, she could learn at least a few lessons from Addie.

Lindsey nodded again and decided not to let Tara upset her anymore. In a few moments, the waiter stepped to their table for their drink orders.

"So, how's the unpacking going?"

"It's not bad at all now. Dakota already unpacked so much for me, I basically only brought the essentials with me this time. I'm already settled in. I even had some extra time last night to play with Lydia."

Living with Sissy came with some major perks for all those involved. She got to spend time with baby Lydia, and Sissy and Tyler were able to steal away for some much-needed sleep or a date.

"Well, that's great. I was going to offer to help, but it sounds like you've got it covered." Addie laughed and pointed at the menu. "I know this sounds silly, but is the chicken salad a salad with chicken on it or is it the chicken and mayonnaise mixture? Sometimes, I can't distinguish between the two when the menu isn't very detailed."

Lindsey's mood lifted, and she laughed at Addie's

observation. "You know, I've thought the same thing at restaurants before. We might have to ask about this one because I love chicken salad, the mixture."

Their drinks arrived, and Lindsey asked, "How are things going for you? Everything going okay?"

Addie's face lit up. "Everything is great. Declan is amazing, and he's incredibly patient with me while I'm going through this big change in my life. School is coming along great. Work is busy. Brian is teaching me to play guitar, and we've been singing at Rusty's every other weekend. Oh, and I forgot to tell you I'll be singing at church this Sunday."

Lindsey clapped her hands together and exclaimed, "Addie! That's amazing. I can't wait to hear you sing."

Addie sighed. "Sometimes, I can't believe this is my life."

Lindsey's phone rang in her purse. It was Sissy.

"Hey, Sis."

"Hey. I'm running a little late. Lydia had a blowout right before I left and it was all hands on deck. I'll be there soon."

Lindsey ended the call and let Addie know Sissy was running late. Kathy and Barbara were still chatting with Ms. Matthews at a table closer to the entrance.

"When do you start work?" Addie knew Lindsey accepted Ian's job offer at the hardware store.

"Monday. Is it weird that I'm really excited about it?"

"Not at all. I was ecstatic when I started my job. I know how much a job can mean to someone."

It was nice to know that at least one person understood that a job that didn't seem glamorous or special to someone else could be incredibly important to her. After spending so much time wondering when her next pay check would fall into place, the consistency of work was a relief.

"I'm ready for you to start work because I'm hoping you'll be a good influence on Ian. Maybe he won't be so grouchy if he doesn't have the stress of work to blame."

They both laughed. It seemed like Addie had picked up on the true Ian in the short months she'd been around. "No pressure, but you're saying I'm in charge of turning the beast into a prince. I'm no Snow White."

"Girl, brush up on your fairy tales. That was Belle."

Barbara and Kathy returned to the table just as Sissy came jogging through the restaurant. "Sorry I'm late. What did I miss?"

Lindsey smiled as her friends and family filled the table, and she couldn't believe the blessings around her. Coming home was the best decision she could've made.

CHAPTER 26

Lindsey

Lindsey dropped her mother off at Barbara's house after lunch and a little more shopping. Although Barbara's house was only a quarter of a mile from Dakota's as the crow flies, she had to drive back down Barbara's long drive and back out onto the road before wheeling back up Dakota's drive.

Lindsey wondered why Dakota hadn't made a connecting road already and decided she could probably guess his reasons. He'd let her in on some of the shame he felt after the wreck, and she could imagine he hadn't been traipsing over to visit family very often if he was ashamed. Shame like that would be enough to coax him to shut people out. Little did he know that Barbara wasn't one to give up on her kin. He was only making it harder for her by insisting on the distance.

She hated every mountain he'd climbed and every battle he'd fought without her. His family cared about him unfalteringly, and she knew that without a doubt.

She only wished he could forgive himself since that was the real crux.

As her car broke through the tree line revealing the stunning home Dakota built, she was awestruck by the beauty again. Would she ever get tired of this place? The leaves were changing colors after the latest cold snap, and the warm colored trees swayed in the autumn breeze below a soft gray sky. It could rain any minute now, judging by the ominous clouds.

She parked in front of the garage and bounded up the stairs to the front door. The thought struck her that one day she wouldn't enter through the front door. Sure, she had a key to the garage and back door now, but if things stayed on the path they were on, this would be her home too.

Dakota told her they needed to leave for their surprise date around 5:00 PM, so she barely stopped to remove her shoes in the foyer. "Hey, Kota. Sorry I'm late," she yelled through the house when she didn't see him.

When silence greeted her, she moved through the house, turning to look this way and that for any sign of him. She looked through the window into the backyard to find Dakota washing his truck. Couldn't he see rain was coming?

She decided to leave her Converses in the foyer as she entered the backyard unobserved. She had an urge to feel the ground beneath her feet. The land that Dakota insisted would belong to her too still didn't feel real sometimes.

The cold mud and grass stuck to her feet, binding her to the cold earth. The shock to her senses sent a wave of energy through her feet, up her legs, and into her chest. Yes, this dirt was a part of her. She could feel it in her soul now.

The spray of the garden hose beat high-pressure water against the doors of the truck that trickled down to join the standing water at her feet. Dakota wore a black T-shirt and jeans, and she wondered how he wasn't cold. The wind was sharp enough to cut like a knife.

He heard her when she was about three feet behind him. He turned and shut off the spray of the hose simultaneously. She could see that his shirt was stuck to him and damp from the mist of the hose.

Dakota's smile was striking. Brilliant white teeth framed by his Georgia tanned skin. Her own grin was undeniably quick to follow.

"What are you doing?" she asked.

"Washing my truck," he replied as if it were completely obvious.

"I can see that." She pushed his shoulder playfully as he advanced on her and wrapped his arms around her waist. "But why?" She looked up at the darkening clouds. "It looks like we're getting rain soon."

She rested her hand on the damp shirt on his chest as he explained. "I needed something to do. I got off work early, and I'm not good at waiting. Besides, I'm about to park this one in the garage, and we'll take the Bronco tonight. This shower is supposed to pass soon, so it won't be a problem for tonight."

"Oh, so we're doing something outside tonight?" She'd been fishing for clues since he mentioned the surprise date yesterday, but he was locked up like Fort Knox when it came to giving away hints.

"You'll find out soon enough."

They were nose to nose now, and the scar on his brow caught her attention. She moved her thumb to trace the reminder of the pain of the past. Of all the scars she'd given him, mentally and physically, this one would forever stare back at her.

The physical scars were the ones she couldn't run away from, but she realized she didn't want to. They were souvenirs of the battles they'd fought, and proof that they'd won. She wanted to look back and know how far they'd come. Looking at his scar now felt like looking down into a valley from the peak of a mountain nestled in the clouds.

The unseen scars were there too, but they healed more completely. They were a constant work in progress receiving treatment daily.

The scars were good. They would forever remind them what was worth fighting for. If he could survive the battles he fought alone, she would stand by his side and fight for their future. They'd come so far.

He didn't pull her hand away when she touched the marred line on his face, and she saw it for what it was—another small victory.

"I love you," she breathed with the resolve of a

soldier. She didn't waver and never would again. He should know her heart.

"Even my scars?"

"Every one."

He kissed her then, and she let her weight be supported by his arms as he held her smaller form. Soon, his unstoppable smile prevented their lips from touching as his lips spread thin over his teeth. He tried to continue the kiss, but the smile that overcame him wouldn't be contained. She let off a laugh that sent her soul flying. Had she ever felt so blissfully happy?

He chuckled as he released her and moved to the truck. "Let me park this in the garage, and I'll meet you inside."

She grabbed the hose and pulled it behind her to the back porch. The grime of the mud squished between her toes as she stopped to spray her feet clean. She thought about the undeniable grit in all relationships. Things weren't always easy, but the muddy times when life knocked you in the dirt were much more bearable if you learned to find the joy in the moment.

She tilted her head toward the heavens and the gentle pelts of the first raindrops splattered on her face. The sprinkle wasn't even enough to dampen her clothes, and she didn't run for the shelter of the house. The smell of earth and the fresh breeze that accompanied the rain poured life into her once again.

Dakota found her standing there just as she decided to come inside. "I was just... appreciating."

He nodded as he extended a hand to her. She took

it, following him inside. The walls of the house muffled the tings of the rain as she closed the door against the onslaught of nature. "I know what you mean."

He pulled her closer to him but didn't make a move to wrap her in his arms. She felt it again, that surge of power she associated with his love and support. She wasn't sure which was louder, her heartbeat or the rain beating a tattoo against the metal roof.

She would never know how to show him her appreciation. His loyalty, hard work, selflessness, support. She was immensely grateful for him in every way. "I love you, Dakota. Thank you for arranging a surprise date to see that movie I've wanted to watch."

He laughed. "If I'm taking you on a surprise date, I'm not choosing a movie. We can do that anytime you *tell* me what you want to see, but you'll have to plant the seed on that one. You like so many different movies, I can't keep up. I'm sure it'll be a musical, if you have anything to say about it."

She rolled her eyes. "Yes, there is a musical I want to see, but I just thought I could guess where we're going."

"Not a chance, but don't worry. You'll love it."

He turned to grab his jacket from the barstool and she noticed a box on the bar. "You've got mail." The box was open, so she wasn't actually letting him know anything new.

He froze for a moment in the process of putting on his jacket. "Yeah, about that..."

She wrinkled her brows and pulled down one flap of the box to peek inside.

It was rose petals. A box *full* of rose petals in pinks, whites, and reds.

Stepping away from the package, she turned to him and saw his look of distaste. "What is..."

"I'm not sure. I already let Jake know about it."

That wasn't much to go on. "What is it, Dakota?" She needed a better answer.

He pushed a breath out in a rush. "I think it's from Tara, but I don't have any way to prove it. There isn't any postage. Whoever sent it put it directly in my mailbox."

"Has she ever sent you anything before?" Her blood pressure was rising. She could feel it in the heat of her face.

"No, but who else would send something so... strange?"

As Lindsey's chest tightened, she recalled the same feeling earlier today. "Wait, I saw her today."

Dakota's eyes widened at the revelation. "Did she say anything, or seem angry?"

"No, but she gave me a sneer. I expected as much. I didn't expect..."

"Yeah." Dakota rubbed the back of his neck. "She hasn't ever caused any real problem before, but I'll admit I also wasn't too worried because it was just me. Now that you're in my life, every move she makes scares me."

"You think it's that bad?"

"I don't know. I just can't lose you again."

She cupped his face and sighed. "This is just one more thing we'll be facing together. Don't worry. She can't separate us." She felt none of the uncertainty from her earlier encounter with Tara now. She could do anything with Dakota beside her.

"Besides, Jake knows about it. Maybe he can question her."

Dakota shook his head. "She didn't actually do anything wrong. He can't just show up at her door accusing her."

He was right. As long as things weren't harmful or held the promise of such, they could handle it.

She smiled and took his hand, leading him to the door. "We're going to have fun tonight. No more thinking about creepy flower boxes. Take me on that surprise date."

CHAPTER 27
Dakota

He could feel her questioning eyes on him as he pulled into the field that served as overflow parking beside the church. It satisfied him immensely that she still looked confused as he parked and jumped out of the vehicle without a word. When he opened her door and extended his hand to her, she didn't grasp it.

"Why are we at the church? Better yet, why are so many people here?" Her love of surprises turned to dislike if she was left to simmer too long in the dark.

"Relax." His slight southern drawl became accentuated as he tried to coax her from the truck. "It's the Fall Festival. Did you forget what day it is?"

He could see the wheels turning in her head as she realized it was Halloween night. Her face lit up in anticipation.

"You're kidding!" She leaped from the truck into

his arms. He held her close and hoped he could always make her this happy.

She'd always been a sucker for festivals and craft fairs. They'd been attending their church's annual Fall Festival since they were kids.

Over the years, the festival only grew in popularity. More parents were willing to take their kids to trunk-or-treat at a church than they were to spend hours walking the streets in the dark. Although, many parents gathered with other families and rode through neighborhoods in trailers filled with hay and pulled by a pick-up truck.

There were games and contests, and he loved seeing Lindsey's competitive side. She wasn't ruthless in her strategy, but she did beat herself up quite a bit for losing.

The cake walk was always her favorite. He could remember multiple years watching her trip over her own feet trying to grab a seat in the musical chairs game, but some of his best memories were of carrying home her winnings of homemade chocolate cake.

"I thought you loved the Fall Festival. Did you think we wouldn't celebrate?"

She was bouncing on her toes as they made their way through the droves of people waiting for the hayride in the parking lot.

"I guess I lost track of time this year. I can't believe it snuck up on me." She was still smiling from ear to ear, and he grabbed her shoulders to pull her in for a kiss on the top of her head as they walked.

Seeing her brimming with this excitement was the best part of his days. What he wouldn't give to keep her in this child-like happiness.

She stopped short beside him, and he turned to see Ms. Miller standing by the ticket booth. Lindsey turned to him and sighed. "I've gotta apologize."

He did an excellent job of containing the chuckle he felt bubbling in his middle. "I know. It's just..." What were they going to tell her? "I need to come with you. I was part of it too."

Ms. Miller turned to them with a sharp scowl that scrunched her lips when she recognized them. "Well, I didn't expect to see you two tonight."

"Ms. Miller, I know you've probably heard by now that I've moved back to town, and I just wanted to make things right between us. I wasn't very nice the last time we ran into each other, and I wanted to tell you I'm sorry. I shouldn't have done that."

"Yeah," Dakota continued, "we shouldn't have made up that story about Lindsey opening a burlesque show in town. We both knew better." He wrapped his arm around Lindsey's shoulder and pulled her closer.

Ms. Miller's chin rose higher in the air. "I can't believe you did that, Dakota Calhoun. You made me look like a fool in front of the preacher, and my sewing group, and my hair stylist, and... well, all my friends."

At least they hadn't been wrong about Ms. Miller spreading the gossip.

Lindsey stepped forward. "I'm sorry, Ms. Miller. It

won't happen again. We do know better than to make things up like that."

The old hag nodded her head as if justice was served. "I heard you'll be keeping the books at the hardware store now. I like that idea much better than a sin trap. You just stay outta trouble and don't tempt Dakota into some of those loose ways you've come into."

Lindsey straightened beside him and drew in a deep, slow breath. "I'll try, Ms. Miller."

"See you later, Ms. Miller." Dakota ushered Lindsey away from the woman as fast as he could.

"Well, that was—"

Lindsey interrupted him. "Not as bad as I expected. I don't know why I didn't do it sooner."

Seeing Lindsey gain her confidence and strength back was its own reward. He watched her rub her hands together in a mixture of excitement and sheer cold as they waited to enter the church with about three dozen others.

He felt a hefty slap on his back just as Brian passed him to wrap Lindsey in a hug. He was about to interfere with Brian's full-on mauling when Marcus appeared at his side. The guy looked like he belonged in a horror flick with his shaggy dark hair and drab clothing.

"He's harmless." Marcus didn't need to lead with a greeting. He wasn't ruled by pleasantries.

She removed Brian's arm but wrapped her own arms around her middle. Dakota wasn't wearing a jacket he could give her, and he knew the night would only get more frigid if they decided to take the hayride.

Dakota wrapped his arms around her as he whispered in her ear, "I'm gonna run to the truck and get your jacket. I'll be right back."

"You don't have to do that. I'll be fine." Of course, she would tough it out. She never asked for anything for herself.

"Be right back."

She linked her fingers behind his neck and pressed her forehead to his as she always did when they parted. Separations were always temporary, and no good-byes were ever needed.

After jogging to the truck in the field to retrieve her jacket, he slowed to a walk and re-entered the huddle of people milling around the trailers and the entrance.

He spotted her from about fifteen feet away. She was easy to pick out of a crowd, even with her small stature. He was drawn to her in a way he couldn't explain, and he knew her by her stance, even though she faced away from him. He moved slower through the crowd just happy to watch her, until she turned and someone stepped between them, partially obscuring his view of her in the yellow light.

His body tensed as he recognized Cody Henderson. When would that guy give it up? He kept an eye on them as he moved through the teeming sea of people. When Cody moved to hug her, he saw the look on Lindsey's face in the moonlight.

She wasn't happy. Her teeth showed, but the smile was anything but genuine and it made him slow the pace of his eager steps to watch the exchange unfold. He knew Lindsey wasn't interested in Cody, but something inside him was drawn to the scene.

Dakota watched as she pulled away, and he was close enough to hear her friendly, but reserved, "Hey." If she looked to her left, she could see him in the crowd.

Cody certainly wasn't aware of his presence behind him as his mind ran with thoughts of Lindsey with another man. What they had was too precious to squander, and he trusted her explicitly. Still, his chest ached at the thought of losing her.

He knew Lindsey was beautiful inside and out. She was a woman to admire, respect, and cherish. He wasn't under any illusion that he was worthy of her attention. She was a rare woman, loyal and selfless, and he would gladly spend the rest of his life working to make sure he could make her happy.

Bringing her to this festival was only one small way he could show her love. He knew Lindsey better than anyone, save Sissy, and he would keep digging and searching for things that would light up that smile on her face.

By the time he reached her side, he heard every word she said to Cody.

"I'm here with Dakota. You know that." It was only a slight reprimand, but he could tell she was tired of reminding Cody of her steady relationship status.

Cody's grin took on a sinister shape he'd never seen before. "Maybe next time."

Dakota's heavy hand landed on Cody's shoulder before his last word. He looked to Lindsey and caught the briefest expression of fear before she composed herself. The last thing he wanted was to see her scared.

"Sorry, Cody, but there won't be a next time." He looked at Cody and kept his hand firmly on the man's shoulder. "She's with me... forever." He gave Cody a pat of dismissal and turned to Lindsey.

Lindsey was all he could see. Her smile was radiant, and she failed at hiding her surprise. "Thank you," was all she mouthed.

"He wouldn't hurt you, but I'll keep putting my foot down for you until he gets the message."

A whistle pierced the night from the first truck causing both of their heads to turn in attention. He handed her the jacket, and she wrapped it around her thin shoulders. "You want to do the hayride first?" she asked.

He motioned toward the trailers. "Lead the way."

They settled into the hay on the last cold night of October. Lindsey nestled into his side, and he felt undiluted pride and love for the strong woman beside him. He'd lived with uncertainties for long enough, and it was time to trust the gift that he'd been given.

He wrapped her in his arms and looked to the star-flecked sky. The collective buzzing of the crowd faded to a muffle as he let himself be consumed by the moment.

He closed his eyes and kissed the top of her head. *God, thank you for this wonderful woman. Thank you for our life together. And thank you for leading me out of the darkness and back to You.*

He wasn't a perfect man, but he wanted to be better every day. God was giving him a second chance. Not just with Lindsey, but almost a second chance at life after allowing him to survive that awful wreck. He couldn't mess up his second chance.

She smiled up at him as the truck began to move in the cool, dark night. They may still have to run a one-man show from time to time, but there was no denying they were in this together now.

CHAPTER 28
Lindsey

Six weeks later

Lindsey sat in her office at the hardware store and tried to force her brain to concentrate on the spreadsheet displayed on the monitor. She swallowed hard and gave in to a glance at the bouquet of flowers on the edge of her desk again. A delivery of pink flowers showed up just after lunch, and she hadn't been able to focus on her work since their arrival.

Why would Dakota send her flowers? Maybe he just needed a way to deliver the message on the card.

She picked up the card and read it again. *Meet me at the barn.*

There wasn't a signature or explanation. Yet, it had to be Dakota.

He could've just texted her. They'd never been a showy couple. They were sometimes too practical for their own good, and she preferred it that way. They never put any emphasis on gifts in their relationship. The way he cherished her was a gift, and her respect for him was her gift in return.

She didn't want to be ungrateful, but the flowers bothered her.

What had her hands sweating now was the fact that Dakota *knew* she didn't like flowers. He'd never once bought her flowers before, and it was because she'd asked him not to.

Aside from the fact that flowers were expensive, the main reason she didn't like them was because they died so quickly. The smell of flowers reminded her of death.

The last funeral she'd attended had been Dakota's dad's, and the only thing she remembered about the service was the overwhelming smell of mourning flowers.

It's strange how a smell can trigger a memory, and right now she remembered Sissy at the funeral. They were so young, and Sissy wasn't able to process the loss. She remembered Sissy's tears falling into her hair and on her shoulders as she supported her friend's body while she cried.

The smell from the corner of her desk wafted toward her now, threatening to suffocate her. She stood and moved the gaudy vase to a small runner table on the other side of the room.

She sat back at her computer, determined to work, when the question bombarded her again, undeniable and unavoidable.

Why would Dakota send those flowers?

She looked back to the vase, resolved to be grateful for the gift. The flowers were truly beautiful. The creamy peonies, cotton candy carnations, snow-white lilies, and enormous hydrangeas were accented with greenery. The result was a pink monstrosity almost too big to carry. The vase was frosted pink glass with a huge fuchsia tulle bow.

He must have told the florist to just send something with the note. Pink was her least favorite color, and Dakota knew as much. They may have been separated for six years, but she hadn't forgotten one thing about Dakota. She still knew everything he liked and disliked. Surely, it hadn't been different for him. Although, she *had* only been back in his life for a few weeks. Maybe he just forgot.

The note wasn't even hand written. It was typed in plain block letters. *Meet me at the barn.*

She wanted to call him, but they made a point not to call each other during working hours unless it was important. She texted him at lunch but didn't receive a response.

The lack of response wasn't unusual. They focused on work during the day and spent the evenings together. They both understood the importance of their jobs, and they had their whole lives to spend together.

She wanted to switch the topic of her thoughts, but she studied the message again. He wanted to meet her at the barn. The place that held so many wonderful memories for both of them.

Suddenly, she wasn't worried anymore. She was excited. What could he possibly be planning? Her breathing picked up, and her pulse quickened. It was a Thursday night, but what did that matter when every night could be date night?

Brian walked in the open door to her office and knocked as an afterthought.

"Hey, pretty lady. Did you send that check?" He stopped and turned toward the flowers with a scowl on his face. "Who sent you flowers?"

She couldn't help but laugh at the way his nose scrunched up as he pointed at the arrangement. Brian wasn't ever serious, so she was used to his crazy reactions.

"They're from Dakota, and yes, I sent the check." She looked at the clock and breathed a sigh of relief when she realized it was time to go home. She turned off her computer, and Brian stood like a statue in the doorway.

"He knows you hate flowers, right?" Brian asked with concern.

Even Brian remembered her aversion to flowers. "I don't necessarily *hate* flowers. I just... don't need gifts to know he cares." That was half the truth, but not the reason why she didn't like flowers.

"Uh-huh. Whatever you say, but those flowers stink." His face relaxed a little, but he still wore a scowl.

"Right?" she whispered. "I can't leave them here because I have to lock the office, and I can't imagine how it would smell if they were stuck in here all night. Besides, no one will see them in here except me."

"Take that thing home. They're not welcome. I'm gonna have to have a talk with your boy." He left with a casual wave to her that ended in a swish under his nose to dispel the smell.

She gathered her jacket and purse before approaching the impending presence in the corner and stuffing the card back into the holder. How was she supposed to get this thing home?

After stuffing the vase into the passenger floorboard of her car, she dialed Dakota's number before starting the engine. She took a moment to catch her breath from the struggle to get the gift snugly into the car while the repeating rings chimed in her ear.

His voicemail picked up after a few rings. He must still be at work. She would see him soon either way. They were supposed to meet at the barn according to the card, and the suspense was eating at her. She couldn't imagine why he would concoct this big of a plan to get her to the barn.

She arrived at his house ten minutes later, and Dakota was nowhere to be found. Telling herself he just wanted their next meeting to be whatever surprise was waiting for her at the barn, she placed the vase of flowers on the kitchen bar and left.

The barn wasn't far from the house, but she opted to drive. It was the middle of December, and she instinctively huddled her jacket tighter each time she stepped outside. She couldn't see the barn from the house due to a cluster of trees that sat between them. Even in the winter when the trees were bare, the remaining trunks and branches were still too thick to see through. Still, she assumed Dakota drove since his truck wasn't at the house.

Her anticipation quickly morphed into confusion as she approached the barn and saw a silver BMW she didn't recognize.

Curiosity spurred her forward, although at a hesitant pace. She parked and got out to investigate the car only to find it unoccupied. There was no one in sight, and a small voice in the back of her mind whispered of mischief.

The realization that Dakota hadn't been the one to send the flowers hit her like a freight train. What was going on? Who wanted to meet her here?

She turned toward the barn entrance and strode in with determination. She enjoyed surprises, but being left this deep in the dark was borderline frightening.

The familiar smell of dirt and old wood momentarily comforted her as she scanned the large opening of the barn. Dust motes floated in the sunset rays that lingered in the early twilight. The lack of remaining daylight sparked urgency in her. She needed to get out of here before dark fell.

She stopped to look around again, but there was

no one here. The barn and the field outside were eerily quiet, but someone had to be nearby. There was a car parked outside. Her uneasy feeling turned to panic, and she ran for the exit.

Lindsey stopped when she saw someone sitting in the bunk next to the door. She couldn't make out who it was, but it certainly wasn't Dakota.

The figure in the shadows didn't move and neither did Lindsey. Something about the controlled stillness of the phantom left her paralyzed.

"Who are you? What are you doing here?" When the person didn't answer, she added, "This is private property."

The shadow stood abruptly, and Lindsey recognized it to be a woman's silhouette.

"I know whose property this is," the person seethed.

Whoever this was, she was mad. She could feel the anger pouring from her. She could see it in her stance. The woman's fists were clenched at her sides.

"This is my boyfriend's property." Lindsey's voice threatened to quiver, but she held strong.

"No!"

With that one yell, Lindsey knew who stood before her. She'd heard that raised voice before, and dread coated her body from head to toe at the realization.

It was Tara. The loud, demanding voice of Tara Hanks stopped her cold.

Tara continued in a high-pitched screech. "He isn't your boyfriend!"

Lindsey could see Tara's whole body shake in anger. "What do you want, Tara?" She felt like she was trapped in a cage with a wild animal.

"I want you to leave," she said without hesitation. "You don't belong here, and you don't belong with him. I do."

The words held so much authority that Lindsey was momentarily shaken. There wasn't a reason for Tara to be this angry with her. It didn't make sense.

"I'm not leaving, Tara. Tell me what this is really about." Lindsey stood her ground, but she walked a fine line between keeping Tara at bay and standing up for herself.

"Fine." It was almost completely dark inside the barn now, but she saw Tara lunge for the door.

Lindsey darted for the exit a moment too late. All the remaining light in the barn was snuffed out as the door closed and Lindsey's whole body fell into the door with the force of her run.

She barely registered the stinging pain in her shoulder as she continued to thrust her entire body at the boarded door. Instinctively, she screamed for help, but it was drowned by the whirling in her ears as her adrenaline hit a peak.

The darkness pressed in around her, and she gasped for breath. She backed away from the door, intent on looking for another way out. She turned in place, but no sign of light directed her to an escape. There'd been an addition to the barn since she left, and she wasn't as sure about the layout as she had once been.

She heard Tara's car start, and another wave of panic wracked her body. No one would know where to find her. Had she mentioned to Brian that Dakota wanted to meet at the barn? She couldn't remember.

She remembered her cell phone and frantically patted the pockets of her pants. She'd been distracted by the strange vehicle and left her phone in the car.

Her teeth chattered and her body shook with cold and adrenaline. She hugged her middle in an attempt to control the jittering of her body. She bent forward and closed her eyes. What was the point when she couldn't see her hand in front of her face? She focused on taking deep breaths. In. Out. In. Out.

Her chest ached and her rhythmic breathing skipped as she inhaled the first deep breath of smoke.

CHAPTER 29
Dakota

Dakota pulled up at his house after work expecting to see Lindsey's car. They met at his house almost every evening after work for dinner or a movie. He hadn't bothered to text her when he left work, since he only had a ten-minute drive home from the current construction site.

He dialed her number as he walked inside. Maybe she decided to go out with Addie after work or Sissy needed her help with Lydia. She could've even stopped by the grocery store. There were lots of places she could be. Why was the seed of worry stirring in his stomach?

Her voicemail picked up as he entered the kitchen and he heard, "Hey, you've reached Lindsey," before disconnecting the call.

He walked into the kitchen and a gaudy, pink flower arrangement sat imposing on the bar. It brought him to a stop as it completely dominated the room, which was quite a feat, since Lindsey had gone a little overboard with Christmas decorations recently.

Lindsey hated flowers, and she despised pink. Whoever bought her these flowers didn't know her at all.

A twinge of fear hit him when he realized he must have missed a special occasion if someone else was sending her flowers. He did some quick calculations and realized it wasn't her birthday or any other gift giving holiday. But why the flowers?

He inspected the arrangement and found an index card with typed print that read *Meet me at the barn.*

Who was she meeting? Surely, the flowers weren't for him, but he couldn't figure out who would be meeting Lindsey at the barn.

An uneasy feeling grew roots in his mind as he paced in the kitchen and tried Lindsey's number again only to receive no answer.

That settled the matter. He couldn't sit in this tauntingly empty house for one more second. He was backing out of the driveway before he knew where he was going.

He stopped at the end of the driveway and looked down the road to the parallel drive leading to the barn. The barn had been in his mind since he saw the word on the card. With his decision settled, he drove recklessly, full of uncertainty and dread. When he topped the dam that pocketed the pond, a silver BMW met him on the one-lane path head-on.

His attention was drawn from the car as he noticed

the faint smoke coming from the barn. His fear was a beating drum in his chest urging him into action. He opened the door before the truck was securely in park. He couldn't bring himself to care about the BMW or the person driving it. They weren't going anywhere until he got some answers.

He ran to the driver's window of the silver car to find a red-faced Tara Hanks. She was hysterical, crying and shaking.

"Where's Lindsey?" He shouted it before her window even cracked. His attention was drawn back to the smoke dancing up from the barn.

He didn't care what Tara was doing here, as long as he could find Lindsey. The urgency in everything had jacked through the roof when he started rejecting the pieces his mind was already putting together.

Tara sobbed and sputtered a garbled, "I'm sorry," and that was all it took. He knew what she'd done, and his blood felt like ice.

He locked eyes on the barn and ran. His target was fixed in his mind—Lindsey. He ran as if his feet could lift him from the ground and deposit him at the door of that burning barn.

He prayed as his boots pounded the dry ground beneath his feet. He wasn't able to form any eloquent request, but *Please let her be okay,* played on repeat in his head. He felt every word in his bones, and he pleaded with everything he had inside him.

He felt so far away from her, and she had precious little time. He ate the distance with his pumping legs and pushed for more speed as the burning smell touched his nose and sparked a fire in his lungs.

There was no way he could lose her. She was everything to him, and he was meant to protect her. He'd failed her so miserably, and his anger spurred him forward.

The flames were consuming the door by the time he reached the barn, and he could see that the front entrance wasn't an escape option. He knew this place like the back of his hand. There was a door on the western wall too. He ran for the other door and grabbed the bar lock with both hands. The metal seared his palms and he jerked his hands back on instinct.

The heat from the flames lit his face on one side as the cold, December wind beat against the other side. Roaring was the only thing that filled his head, and he couldn't think straight.

He shucked his jacket off and wrapped his hands in the thick material before tugging the lock free and opening the double doors. Smoke billowed out in waves, pushing him back from the heat.

"Lindsey!" His lungs protested against the smoke filling them, but he couldn't see anything through the gray darkness.

He locked in on Lindsey's car parked in the grass beside the barn and prayed the keys were in it. He jumped in and positioned the car facing the barn and turned the headlights on bright.

He jumped from the car and knelt to the ground.

He was crawling into the scorching building before he could think twice.

Giving up on breathing, he focused on the headlights shining as welcoming as a blessing inside the barn. The flames were roaring loud, but he called for her anyway.

"Lindsey!" He continued to yell as he crawled below the smoke and scoured the barn for her. He moved into the beams of the headlights and spotted her in the middle of the room knelt with her hands over her head beneath the living smoke.

He moved as fast as lightning, crawling on hands and knees through the dirt toward her. He grabbed her up and hoisted her into his arms before she even saw him. Her arms grabbed at his shoulders as he carried her as low as he could beneath the smoke ceiling.

His panic eased a fraction as he strode through the field, away from the barn, with Lindsey in his arms. He hugged her so tight she coughed, and he remembered to give her room to breathe.

Once they were safely away from the barn, he laid her in the grass and pulled her face into his hands. Dirty tear stains ran down her soot-covered face, and his chest tightened for her. A sob jarred her body, and he felt helpless.

He could have lost so much today, but she could have lost more. She could have lost her life, everything that mattered.

Dakota moved her hair away from her face to inspect her further. "Can you hear me, baby? Tell me you're okay, Lindsey." It wasn't a request. He needed to hear her say she was going to be okay.

She nodded her head slightly, and that was good enough for him. He hugged her to his chest again and stilled as her fingers grasped the material of his thick shirt. The smell of smoke was heavy around her, but he couldn't pull away.

He heard Tara's hysterical screams over the roar of the fire, and he was pulled back to reality. He was going to have to deal with so many other things soon, but he couldn't leave Lindsey.

He pulled his cell from his pocket and called Jake who answered on the second ring.

"Hey, man—"

"The barn is on fire, and Lindsey is hurt. Can you get a paramedic and the fire department here? The drive to the barn is blocked by my truck and Tara's car, so you'll have to direct them in through my drive and the trail from the house."

"Got it, boss." Jake knew how to make things happen and knew how to direct the caravan to their off-the-beaten-path location.

"Oh, and I'm pretty sure Tara just tried to kill Lindsey."

Jake spat, "You've gotta be kidding me," before disconnecting the call.

When Dakota turned his full attention back to Lindsey, she was shaking from the cold and her sweat dampened body. Apparently, she must have shed her jacket at some point in the barn because the sweater she wore was too thin for the frigid, winter weather. He released her long enough to remove his pullover and laid it over her torso. He was wearing an undershirt, and the adrenaline was still pumping through his veins, lighting them on fire.

Lindsey coughed, and he turned to her again. "It's all right, Lindz. Jake's sending help." He brushed her hair back and cradled her head to his chest.

Her voice was a jagged rasp, like metal being dragged over rocks. "I'm sorry," she coughed. "I'm sorry the barn is gone."

"I don't care about the barn. I thought I was losing you." He could hear the tremor in his voice, but he didn't care. "And it felt like dying." She should know the truth of what he would be without her light in his life.

"But that was your place... your home."

She coughed again, and he wished he could make her understand. "If anything, it was *our* place. You are my home, and my place is beside you. That's all I need."

He heard the circular wail of the fire engine as it approached, but he couldn't break his attention from Lindsey. He stroked her cheek and was completely certain he'd never been so grateful for anything in his life as he was for her.

Soon, the emergency teams would swarm this acre like ants. Right now, he wanted to savor his last minute alone with her. The orange light from the burning barn cast an eerie shadow over her face. He would do anything to keep Lindsey safe, but he knew this time he had to leave the justice to Jake and his department.

No, he couldn't go after Tara himself. The peaceful future he still envisioned for them could happen if he let the authorities take care of Tara. He wasn't the judge, and he needed some time to process what she'd done. If he'd known sooner the horrors she was capable of, he would've been more cautious.

He looked at Lindsey and all that he still held in his arms. They were both alive and still capable of pursuing all those things if Lindsey would still have him after he brought this disaster upon her.

The flames of the fire behind him masked the red and blue flashes of the police cars and fire engines approaching. In the sea of fire surrounded by the void of night, all he could do was hope their future wasn't turning to ashes in front of him. He prayed she still trusted him to protect her because he would make sure nothing ever harmed her again.

CHAPTER 30
Lindsey

Time had crept at a snail's pace since the fire. Almost four months had passed since she'd been trapped in that barn, and some days, the memories were still hard to shake. A flash of light, a scent of burning wood, or a dark room still sent Lindsey's heart racing.

Lindsey was released from the hospital the day after the fire, but her recovery hadn't stopped there. For weeks after the burning night, she could still feel lingering claw marks in her lungs from the smoke inhalation. Dakota experienced his own degree of lung pain as well. The bright side was the doctor's prognosis, and it kept her optimistic.

You'll make a full recovery.

Those words meant more to her than she ever thought they would. She had her life, and that was more than she thought she would have during those terrible minutes she was trapped in the barn.

Dakota was still reluctant to leave her side, but she continued to reassure him she could manage on her own. His fussing over her was admirable, but unnecessary. The road back to "normal" was long and tiring, but she was getting there... in her own sweet time. Still, it was nice to know he would truly stand beside her during the tough times just as he would in the happy times.

She couldn't think about that time in the barn. For one, it was all a haze in her memory. All she knew was that she hoped to never find herself in a situation so impossible and potentially fatal as that one again.

It was enough to make her wish she could wipe the moments from her memory. She wanted to erase them, get them out of her head. Some days it seemed impossible to force her mind to think of anything else. During those times when she battled the memories, she also fought the tears. But Dakota, Sissy, and Addie were always close by to pull her up and keep her moving forward.

Not to mention her relationship with God was better than ever. The last thing she remembered from those terrifying moments in the barn was praying—praying for a way out, praying for forgiveness, praying for Dakota and what slippery slope he might face if she were hurt or worse.

Today, she walked alone toward her destination in downtown Carson. Dakota knew why she insisted on doing this alone every week. The sun shone brightly on the pale-gray sidewalk, but she preferred to keep her head down to the late March wind. Bird songs and children's laughter tumbled in the spring air, but she couldn't bring herself to enjoy the scene just now. It felt... out of place.

She stopped for the second time, feeling lost and left behind as the cars kept racing past her. Life was bustling around her, but she stood still—brokenhearted. She was a statue on the pavement. As stagnant as an insect frozen in an amber tomb.

Could she do this again? After another deep breath, she resumed her forward movement. She was only a few steps from the entrance to the Cherokee County Jail, and she couldn't stop now. Her heart propelled her forward as her anxiety held her back.

A month after the fire, a letter arrived in the mail at Tyler and Sissy's house addressed to her from a local attorney. An inmate named Tara Hanks requested an audience with her. The letter stated that Tara requested Lindsey come alone and on her own time.

Lindsey had just celebrated her first Christmas at home in six years when the letter arrived. It was hard to piece through the pain that still burned in her lungs, the headaches that felt like her skull could crack from the inside out, and the emotional roller coaster she couldn't climb off.

Lindsey still didn't know how she felt about everything that happened. Sometimes, when the pain was unbearable, she was furious with Tara. But when the ache in her chest and her head was tolerable, her heart ached. After that first visit to the Cherokee County

Jail, that pain that was born of emotion only became stronger and more difficult to understand.

Now more than ever, she realized just how important it was to have a support group. Dakota's family was her own. They'd always been her family, and the connection felt as thick as any blood bond.

Her family was invaluable in her recovery, but there were many nights she sat alone wondering who Tara was leaning on.

The first time she visited Tara, she was terrified. But after coasting through the Christmas season in confusion and anger, she knew she couldn't let it continue. She was furious with Tara for many reasons, but she had to know if seeing her would help the healing. She'd hoped that this last-ditch effort would heal her wounded spirit.

Many visits later, she knew Tara was speaking with a counselor, but their sessions were confidential. Tara was showing quite a bit of growth, and talking with someone seemed to be the one thing she needed.

Lindsey reached the door and time seemed to slow as she entered the imposing building that housed the county jail and sheriff's department. She checked in at the desk in the main lobby and took a seat to wait for summoning. A solitary peace lily sat in the corner beside the check-in desk, seeming lonely and displaced. She turned away from the depressing sight and hugged her jacket tighter around her.

Tara had been investigated for arson and found guilty. The perusal hadn't lasted long, since Tara confessed to setting the fire in the hopes of injuring or killing Lindsey. Tara told the authorities she'd hoped to distance herself from the fire, and no one would be able to link the events to her. Jake said she hadn't even defended herself during the interrogation; she just spilled her entire, feeble plan.

Lindsey was startled from her introspection when a male voice called her name. It echoed through the cavernous stone room as her heart calmed to the slightly elevated pace it had kept since she left home.

Following a faceless man in uniform, she passed through a series of doors punctuated by buzzers and clicks. There were keypad codes to be entered and identification to be verified, but she passed through the building in a daze. The farther into the stone structure she traveled, the more suffocated she felt.

At last they entered a hallway to find Jake waiting in front of a nondescript door she knew all too well—a replica of the dozens of others that dotted the walls. Concern showed plainly on his face, and she breathed a relieved sigh. She would never find herself alone and without friends here. There hadn't been a moment when she forgot just how lucky she was to have friends.

"Hey, Lindz. Are you sure you're okay with this?" He hugged her tight, and she kept silent. His uniform was bulky and starched stiff, but the gesture was comforting just the same. He saw her before and after every visit, and Jake knew just how much these visits took out of her.

He pulled back and looked from her to the door beside them.

"I think I'm ready," she whispered. Coming here was always hard, but the reward was worth anything she had to go through.

Jake knew she was scared, but she silently thanked him for not trying to talk her out of this again. She needed encouragement, not doubt, or she would never be strong enough to continue to face Tara.

"You'll be fine. You've made it this far, and she can't hurt you anymore." He looked away from her as he reminded her, "She's really doing better."

She wondered how many times Jake had said those same words to those who found themselves on the dirty end of crimes. He had a way of soothing stressful situations, which came in handy, since he certainly found himself in the middle of them quite often in his line of work.

Looking down, she mumbled, "I know," as she picked at her fingernails absentmindedly.

"I'll be right here if you need me."

"Thanks, Jake."

As he opened the door for her, the opening felt like a step into a hole—dark and full of so much remorse. She entered the cold room and turned to find Jake standing at the door, his friendly eyes reminding her that she wasn't alone.

She suddenly didn't want to back out. She needed to do this for herself, but she needed to be strong for others too. Her friends stood behind her through everything, but Dakota had been her rock. She wanted to leave here and tell him she'd been strong enough to face her fears again.

When Jake closed the door, she turned back to the room that felt more like a cage. A boxy wooden chair faced a glass wall from desk height up with a circular voice barrier in the center.

Before she'd completely calmed and grown accustomed to her decision to stay, Tara was escorted into an identical room on the opposite side of the glass partition.

Tara's dark hair hung loose and plain around her bare face, but she was still strikingly beautiful. Her high cheekbones needed no blush, and her long, dark lashes were curled perfectly despite the lack of mascara. She looked like a peacock in a desert as she held her shoulders back and her chin high. Her uniform was a dingy gray, but she wore it like a runway model.

Suddenly, she felt at peace and drew comfort from knowing she'd made the right decision to come today. She just needed to see Tara's face. Lindsey knew Tara now. She liked to think she knew the real Tara now—the one not many others could see. There was a different person behind those sharp, beautiful features.

They were left alone but not unheard as Tara took her seat, and she remembered sitting in front of Tara during their first meeting. She hadn't cared what Tara wanted to say. It was a fool's errand. Now, she knew the truth, and it had set her free.

"Thank you for coming." Tara inspected her fingernails for a moment. "I wasn't sure you would."

"I'm here." Lindsey gave her the same soft smile she might give a discouraged child.

"Thank you." Tara reached out her hand, but the glass divided them. There would always be a barrier between them, but things were easier now.

"*Outlander* was good this week." Tara leaned forward and listened to every word as Lindsey tried her best to describe the episode in detail, stopping to elaborate when Tara asked questions or offered her opinion on the dramatics.

They had fallen into a system. Tara missed her favorite premiere television shows, and Lindsey had agreed to keep her updated... for a trade.

"Now," Lindsey propped her elbows on the table and leaned closer, "your turn."

Tara's shoulders lifted and sank deep as she readied herself. "It was a tough one, but it was good."

"Tell me about it."

"Well, it was about Esther."

Lindsey gave Tara a book full of devotionals and in-depth studies of the strongest women in the Bible. Every week, Tara was to recount what she read during their meeting.

Tara's head hung low as she studied the hands in her lap. "She was so selfless," she whispered.

Lindsey felt a stinging in her nose and a lump in her throat as she nodded. "I know."

"Lindz, I could never be like that. I'm trying, but Esther's story made me feel... so small."

"Hey," Lindsey raised her voice to grab Tara's attention. "You can do anything, and you've come so far."

Tara bit her lip. "You make me feel like I really can do anything." Her eyes took on a glassy haze, and Lindsey fought back her own tears. These meetings were always emotionally draining, but now she knew how important it was to help someone like Tara.

During their first meeting, Lindsey was still debating whether coming had been the best idea when Tara began. "I owe you an explanation. I've learned a lot about myself since I came here, and you deserve to know that I'm sorry."

It was the first time she witnessed Tara speak with any real conviction, and she hadn't known if she should trust it. Either way, the stark apology infuriated Lindsey instead of absolving Tara.

Lindsey's anger was still so raw, she hadn't been able to contain it. "You're sorry. Is this part of a twelve-step program they put you on for an early release?" Her pitch rose, and she leaned forward, hands gripping the small shelf before her. "You're sorry!"

"I can't take back what I did. Honestly, I don't know what I was thinking. I was... overwhelmed by things... emotions, I didn't understand."

"You're saying you're not old enough to know better, Tara?" Lindsey spat.

"No. I am. But I lived a life for myself for so long, it

seemed... normal to do whatever I should to get the things I wanted."

Lindsey just stared at her, but Tara kept her head down in a shameful pose.

When Tara looked back up, her face was rose-red and her bottom lip trembled. "My dad died."

They sat still for a moment as the tick of the clock stabbed at the silence, absorbing the enormity of the death brought to life between them.

"He was all I had. My mom killed herself when I was young, and Dad wasn't the best, but he was all I had."

Tears rolled down Tara's face, and Lindsey knew they were genuine. She hated those tears and the truth they represented.

"He wasn't awful to me, but he kept me at arms' length. He was the nicest man, but he wouldn't let me in. I know he loved me, but he didn't know how to show it. I was just a little girl when Mom died, and he didn't know how to raise me on his own. Neither of us was good at expressing our feelings, and it just... continued when I became an adult.

"My dad died about three years ago. I didn't know how to process the loss because I didn't know how I felt about him. I could've hated him just as easily as I loved him, for all I knew. Sometimes, I felt both extremes in the same breath."

She'd watched as Tara wiped the tears from her face and wondered where this dive into her history would end.

"I ran into Dakota for the first time the week my dad died."

Here it was. The connection. Lindsey's throat constricted, and she was sure she would suffocate if Tara continued.

"Tara, I…"

"Dakota was different from anyone I'd ever met, except my dad. He was good and kind, but he kept pushing me away. My dad was the only person who ever treated me that way, and he was the only person in this world I knew truly loved me."

She could feel her face heating with the realization that Tara misunderstood love because she'd never been shown love. Lindsey covered her face with her hands but couldn't hide the sorrow.

"I'd heard the rumors. I knew it was your fault. The reason he wouldn't love me. You broke his heart."

Lindsey felt the bile rise in her throat. Tara was talking about her Dakota and the hurt she'd caused him. She fought tooth and nail to forgive herself for causing him so much pain, and hearing about that time when he'd been lost tore at her insides.

"I saw a piece of myself in him. He was just as broken as I was. I heard about the wreck. Someone in a one car collision too drunk to know his own name is a man with a death wish. But I was too caught up in myself to even consider anyone else."

Tara sobbed into her hands, and Lindsey just stared at her, unable to breathe.

Tara's words were garbled and punctuated in the

wrong places by heaves and sobs. "No one has ever cared about me the way he cares about you. I chose the one person who couldn't love me and locked myself into a pretend relationship tainted by my messed-up ideas about affection. I know that now. I'm seeing a counselor, and I understand things now that I didn't before."

Tara took a moment to compose herself as her emotional outburst died down.

"I shouldn't have cared that Dakota didn't love me. I didn't love him either, not really. I wanted someone to care about me, and for some reason I didn't blame him for his lack of feelings for me. I blamed you. You had everything while I had nothing, and it seemed unfair."

She began to understand Tara in that moment. Tara had continued an immature relationship with her father until the day he died. No wonder Tara was afraid to form relationships with other people. What if no one ever loved her more than her father?

Then, when her father was gone—the only connection she'd ever known—she sought out a replica. Someone nice to push her away was exactly what she found in Dakota.

"When you came back, I saw the end of my crutch. I craved a connection, any connection, but everyone here knows me, and they hate me."

How could she respond to that? She felt strongly toward Tara, but surely not everyone felt the same.

Then she thought of the way Tara used to cut

down everyone else in high school with her cold attitude. If she treated everyone that way, no wonder she hadn't found anyone who loved her.

"I felt trapped and bound by the connection I had to Dakota, the only person who didn't outright shun me. I've never had friends. Ever. I've talked to the counselors here, and they helped me see that I didn't cultivate a healthy relationship with him from the start. He was honest with me about how he felt, and I didn't listen. I was dependent on the strangled emotions I created, and when I made a plan to get him back, I didn't care that you would get hurt. I saw you as a thief, but that's not what you were at all. I can see it now, and I'm sorry."

Lindsey didn't speak, but a tear ran down her own face at Tara's confession. Tara was confused and unloved in so many ways. Her earlier words rang back at her.

You're saying you're not old enough to know better, Tara?

Normally, Tara *was* old enough to know better, but she'd grown up without love. Our experiences mold us, they form us into the people we will continue to be as we grow.

Tara's trembling sobs started up again. "I can't believe I did this. I'm so sorry. I wish I could take it back."

She knew Tara's apology was genuine. She hadn't once mentioned the poor conditions she was forced to endure in the jail or her own discomfort. She'd given Lindsey what she promised—answers.

Lindsey reached out and touched the glass as if she could place her hand on Tara's shaking shoulder. "Tara," she whispered, and she waited for acknowledgement.

When the worst of Tara's lament passed, she looked back at Lindsey with red, puffy eyes. She held Tara's stare and said, "I forgive you."

Tara tilted her head in confusion and her eyes narrowed. "I didn't ask you here for forgiveness. I don't think I deserve it. I wanted you to know where I was and what I'm working toward. I know that what I did was wrong. I want you to be able to enjoy the happiness I've never known because I know better now. What I don't know is how you can forgive me."

Lindsey nodded. "I just hope it helps you find what you're looking for to know that I'm not your enemy. I think I understand you, and I hate that you had to endure so much. I hope you can heal from what's been done to you. If I forgive you, maybe I can start to heal myself too. I came here today to learn things *from* you, but I ended up learning *about* you. Thank you for that."

"I hope I can be worthy of your forgiveness someday."

"We're all a constant work in progress, Tara, but I want you to know that you can have the love you're looking for."

"I—I don't understand."

Lindsey spent the remainder of their first visit telling Tara about God's unfailing love for His children. It was one of the most important conversations she'd ever been a part of, and she knew that Tara was the reason God led her back to Carson.

After the first visit with Tara, Lindsey was so torn up, she prayed for most of the next week. Tara's gut-wrenching story hadn't left her mind, and she knew her work with Tara wasn't finished.

The next week, she visited again, but she didn't ask to know any more about Tara's past. Sometimes, Tara offered insights into more of her regrets or struggles, but Lindsey didn't push her. They began praying together, and Lindsey asked Jim Pearson, the preacher at church, to visit Tara too. Soon, she was able to understand why Lindsey forgave her.

Lindsey gave Tara the book on their third meeting, and they'd been talking about it every week since. The time she spent with Tara was often therapeutic for both of them. She couldn't change Tara's sentence, but she hoped Tara could make the best of the future that lay before her.

When she left Tara that day, Lindsey felt strangely altered standing in the midday sun on the streets of downtown Carson. The same sun fell on her shoulders, but it felt warm and comforting amidst the cool spring air where it was muted and stifling before entering the building earlier. She pulled her jacket tighter around her body and took a moment to look around.

This was her home, and she didn't question her path now. She was meant to be here in this moment, and she knew she was incredibly blessed. Her home, her family, and her friends were all in one place. Now that she saw with her own eyes that Tara was making progress, her heart was at peace here.

The town felt the same and different in its own ways. Collectively, the town was stuck in time, but the people were growing, changing pieces that kept things moving forward.

She hadn't realized she was searching for a home when she arrived here almost six months ago for Lydia's birth, but she found that elusive treasure just the same. This was always her home, but she was too ashamed to admit it before. Carson and the people here had a way of reminding her who she really was. She felt like her dreams flourished here naturally, and hope was all around her.

CHAPTER 31
Lindsey

Lindsey stormed into the house and yelled, "Dakota!" as she stomped through the kitchen and threw her keys on the counter.

The door leading to the back yard flew open with a bang, and Dakota stood framed in sunlight. "What's wrong? What happened?"

He didn't hesitate. He closed the gap between them and wrapped her in his arms before she could answer. He was always on edge when she visited Tara. She often spent those mornings assuring him she would be fine, while he toed the line between being supportive and letting her know she didn't have to go.

"Nothing's wrong. I did it. I saw her, and I'm... fine. Actually, I'm better than fine. She's really doing great."

He sighed and released her. "I'm incredibly proud of you, Lindz. You're doing something amazing by helping her."

She knew he worried about her visits with Tara, but they both knew she didn't have a choice. Tara needed her, and she didn't have it in her to say no.

Lindsey pulled back to look at him and felt the familiar and friendly butterflies in her stomach. She would always be in awe of him—her rock, her support team, her *person*—the one she could always count on.

The love she felt for him made fireworks seem dim. How lucky was she to be loved by a man who was the total package? Dakota was smart, funny, selfless, honest, and loyal, and she would never take him for granted. She'd hit the love jackpot.

She met his gaze with pride as she wanted him to see the truth in her eyes. "I'm really okay. She's helping me too." Lindsey rubbed her hands over his shoulders as she spoke. "I feel better now that I'm seeing her. I'm sorry I haven't dealt with this very well, but I can feel things changing. I feel closer to my old self." Her fingers stroked over his worried cheek as she smiled.

The gesture was strong enough to ease his creased brow. "Good," he breathed and pulled her back into his embrace. "Do you want to talk about it?"

She wanted to tell him everything, but the things Tara shared with her felt too personal. Still, Tara's actions had changed his life too, and he deserved some inkling of the closure she'd been gifted.

"Tara had a hard life, and sometimes the people we meet have a stronger impact on us than we expect. I think she needed time to move away from the hurt she was feeling so she could focus on finding peace in her own life. I've forgiven her, and I hope you can too someday."

He stopped stroking her back, but overall kept his composure. "I trust you, Lindz. I think I've already forgiven her. The way you talk about her now has really resonated with me."

She kissed his cheek and kept her smile. She would never demand he forgive Tara, but she was overjoyed that he'd come to the decision on his own and could begin to feel the peace she knew now. She even wished the same for Tara.

He cupped her face in his calloused hands that dwarfed her small features. "I've missed that smile, Lindz. You don't know how amazing it is to see you happy again."

"I'm sorry it's taken me so long."

"Will you wait right here? I have a surprise for you."

He ran down the hallway, leaving her giggling in the kitchen. Ten seconds later, his lengthy stride carried him back to her sporting a huge ear-to-ear grin, but she didn't see a surprise.

He stopped in front of her and paused long enough that she got a little too anxious and bounced on the balls of her feet. "Well..." She was going to burst with excitement if he didn't hurry.

His eyes never left hers as he sank to his knee before her. A gasp of air filled her lungs as she saw the small box in his hand. Immediately, she sank to her own knee, and he protested.

"No, Lindz..."

"Stand up with me. Even for this." Her vision grew blurry, but she kept her composure. She'd never been surer of anything in her life. Grabbing his hands, she pulled him up. "I'm honored to stand beside you."

He held her hands tightly, and she even detected a slight tremor in his grasp. "I meant to ask you at Christmas, but I wanted to give you time to deal with the things that happened. Now, seeing you happy like this just feels right. I can't wait another day to tell you that you're my world. I love you more every day, every second, and I want to spend the rest of my days with you. Will you marry me?"

"Yes! Always, yes." Her arms wrapped around him and she buried her face in his neck.

She hadn't expected to find herself so happy. Even if the road was paved in heartache, she would do it all over again for this moment.

Their hearts were fused together in irreversible ways long ago. She belonged to him before a ring ever encircled her finger. Her vows were etched on her heart, and they would stay there, unfaltering, forever. But declaring their love in front of God and the people who loved them was the last step in completing the life they always wanted... together.

She thought the entertainment business was her trial by fire, but it wasn't. Enduring life without Dakota had been her fire, and now the true fire had melded them together forever.

There was no turning back from this one. They'd

been primed by their separation, thrust back together, then forged by the flames and emerged a malleable, single entity incapable of separation. Alchemy had its redeeming qualities when beauty could be formed from ashes. First, everything has to burn down.

She pulled back so she could link her arms behind his neck and rest her forehead against his. What had once been a silent way to leave now felt like a vow—a promise of a life waiting to be lived together.

Other Books By Mandi Blake

Blackwater Ranch Series

Complete Contemporary Western Romance Series

Remembering the Cowboy

Charmed by the Cowboy

Mistaking the Cowboy

Protected by the Cowboy

Keeping the Cowboy

Redeeming the Cowboy

Blackwater Ranch Series Box Set 1-3

Blackwater Ranch Series Box Set 4-6

Blackwater Ranch Complete Series Box Set

Wolf Creek Ranch Series

Complete Contemporary Western Romance Series

Truth is a Whisper

Almost Everything

The Only Exception

Better Together

The Other Side

Forever After All

Love in Blackwater Series

Small Town Series

Love in the Storm

Love for a Lifetime

Unfailing Love Series

Complete Small-Town Christian Romance Series

A Thousand Words

Just as I Am

Never Say Goodbye

Living Hope

Beautiful Storm

All the Stars

What if I Loved You

Unfailing Love Series Box Set 1-3

Unfailing Love Series Box Set 4-6

Unfailing Love Complete Series Box Set

Heroes of Freedom Ridge Series

Multi-Author Christmas Series

Rescued by the Hero

Guarded by the Hero

Hope for the Hero

Christmas in Redemption Ridge Series

Multi-Author Christmas Series
Dreaming About Forever

Blushing Brides Series
Multi-Author Series
The Billionaire's Destined Bride

About the Author

Mandi Blake was born and raised in Alabama where she lives with her husband and daughter, but her southern heart loves to travel. Reading has been her favorite hobby for as long as she can remember, but writing is her passion. She loves a good happily ever after in her sweet Christian romance books and loves to see her characters' relationships grow closer to God and each other.

Acknowledgments

There are so many hearts that are involved in the production of a book. The writer is the first to contribute, but certainly not the last.

I want to thank my friends and family for standing by me when I decided to write books. I couldn't have written the first word without their support, and I'm blessed to be surrounded by people who motivate me to push for more in this career.

My friend Angela Watson has always stood by me. She makes sure I'm motivated, she feeds my inspiration, and nudges me to keep going. Not many people find a friend like her, and I'm honored to know her.

My editor, Brandi Aquino, has certainly shaped this work, and I'm glad we found each other. This book wouldn't be what it is without her.

Amanda Walker designed the stunning cover of this book, and I appreciate everything she does to make it look good.

I owe a huge thanks to Ginny, Tanya, and Lyssa who gave wonderful feedback and made this book better with every bit of advice they gave. My author friends, K. Leah and Jeanine Hawkins, have helped me navigate this new business. I'm incredibly blessed to work alongside others who are willing to help me grow as a writer. Thank you for your guidance!

I'm honored you've chosen to take a chance on this book, and I hope it exceeds your expectations. If you enjoy the book, please consider leaving a review on Amazon, Goodreads, or any platform you choose. Your opinion matters, and I take each review to heart.

Note from the Author

Once again, I find myself writing flawed characters. They never start out this way, but real people are full of scars. It's only fitting that the characters we read about in books are the same.

Sometimes, the hero isn't perfect, but I hope you found the message of hope as you read this book. We all make mistakes, and people battle invisible foes every day. Fortunately, our characters find that overcoming obstacles is possible with God and the people who love us.

The scary thief of joy in this book is alcoholism, and it can be a soul-crusher. The worldly things that draw us away from God are never as glamorous as they first seem. The killing blow to many relationships comes from a false friend.

Never Say Goodbye is the story of Dakota and Lindsey as they search for a place to call home and find healing in forgiveness. I hope you enjoyed reading this story as much as I loved writing it.

Living Hope
UNFAILING LOVE SERIES BOOK THREE

Natalie Burke trudges through life in a daze of work and tending to her ailing mother. Every day is a fight to keep a roof over their heads. She doesn't have time to date when she works two jobs.

Deputy Jake Sims lives his life to protect others. When the amber-eyed beauty captures his attention at a crime scene, he wants nothing more than to help her. Too bad she's pushing him away at every turn.

After Natalie loses her mother, Jake makes a vow to help her overcome her grief and get back on her feet. Just as their relationship begins to grow, they discover Natalie's problems have only just begun.

Will Jake be able to rescue Natalie, or will he be too late to save the woman who stole his heart?

Made in the USA
Columbia, SC
18 March 2025

55343361R00178